REVIEWS

"Don't start reading in bed if you're planning to get any sleep. Richard Alan Hall has written a fast-paced, intricately woven plot, with an ending that will keep you checking to see when the next book comes out."

Dean Robb, attorney and author
Cindy Robb, avid reader
Suttons Bay, Michigan

"It's never wrong to do the right thing," asserts one of the main characters in Richard Alan Hall's new novel, *For Better Or Worse*. The right thing, in this case, is to rush out and buy Hall's book and become schooled in the art of Good vs. Evil.

Our heroes on white horses this time around are Cuban Special Forces and the 'True Believers,' who combine high-tech weaponry with small town smarts to outwit an international crime syndicate that threatens those near and dear to Stanley McMillen of Big Bay. (And that, my friends, is something you never, ever want to do.) Heartbreaking, gut-wrenching, uplifting and joyful, *For Better Or Worse* proves the Bible verse that darkness cannot overcome light."

Jim Rink
Editor of *American Wine Society Journal*

"This story weaves a web of unconditional, simple and pure love, where hearts beat in unison. And an evil that is so gut wrenching, it will make you sit up and think. It's all about the journey, about people and not just the destination. The human trafficking and politics involved is sickening; who's in who's pocket. And mosquito virus…oh my gosh, I almost jumped right out of my chair. This novel is riveting. I couldn't put it down. Exquisitely written… *For Better Or Worse* should be on the top of your 'must-read' list."

Barbara A. Ely
Rockford, Michigan

"In Richard Alan Hall's fourth novel, *For Better Or Worse*, I found that I was just pulled in and couldn't stop reading. In fact, I finished it in one sitting. Through Richard's stories within stories and tales within tales, we experience adventure, love, compassion, true brotherhood, and a dedication to doing what's right. As Mr. Hall pens twice in this novel, "It's never wrong to do the right thing." I found myself inspired. Thank you, Richard Alan Hall for sharing your gift, and the beautiful way you put the words together in your exciting, powerful and uplifting novels."

Y. Patrick Mazor, Author
Amarillo, Texas

"Another magnificent adventure…so captivating and transformative. Before you know it you've been through a whirlwind of horror and not once did you ever doubt love. If you don't already believe, read Richard Alan Hall's Big Bay novel, *For Better Or Worse;* it will transform you into a 'True Believer.'"

Brenda DeNoyer Girolamo, Artist and Author
Derry, New Hampshire

Other novels by Richard Alan Hall

BIG BAY NOVELS

Remarkable
Seldom As They Seem
No Gray Twilights

RICHARD ALAN HALL

FOR BETTER OR WORSE

A BIG BAY NOVEL

rah books
KEEP IT UNDER YOUR HAT PUBLISHER

Designed by Saxon Design, Inc, Traverse City, MI

Printed in the United States of America

To contact the author, email: rahall49684@gmail.com
Author's website: RichardAlanHall.net
Visit the author's Facebook page at: Richard Alan Hall-Author

To order additional signed copies, call Big Bay World Headquarters
(Horizon Books, Traverse City) @ 800-587-2147

For my friend, Doctor Daniel Bonifacio.

ACKNOWLEDGEMENTS

Thank you, Angela Saxon of Saxon Design
for designing this book and cover.

Thank you, Lisa Mottola Hudon. You have once again
done the hard work. You make me a better writer.

Thank you, Jill Beauchamp for your invaluable assistance.
You have made this a better book.

Thank you, Jim Rink, for your insight and suggestions.

Thank you, Jill Johnson Tewsley.
You are an amazing publicist. I am astounded.

Thank you, Angel Burke for taking the
perfect picture on the back cover.

Thank you, Debra Jean Hall. This is your fault, again.

And thanks always to our Eternal Daddy.

Table of Contents

PROLOGUE

A dream is not merely a wish.
An idea becomes a dream when we believe
and our hearts are filled with hope.

Richard Alan Hall

CHAPTER 1

EUPHORIC SMILE

Doctor A.W. Blue practiced medicine in Big Bay for nearly twenty years before he left on a Saturday night. He simply closed the office, made evening rounds at Big Bay General, and then drove to Key West in the company of Rita, his office nurse. A kind and gentle man, he did this to divert attention away from his wife who was having a series of sexual affairs with several men stationed at Coast Guard Station Big Bay. He blamed himself for being absorbed in his practice and not paying proper attention to the woman he adored. A.W. and Rita stayed at the La Concha Hotel on Duval Street for eleven months.

When a private detective hired by his wife finally tracked them down, demanding more money, Doctor Blue and Rita fled to Cuba with the help of a friend they had met at the Green Parrot bar. Quinn O'Malley took them to a barrier island off the north coast of Cuba called Cayo Coco. When Quinn O'Malley told his college buddy, Fidel Castro, that A.W. was a physician, the Cuban government opened a health clinic on the island. A.W. and Rita saw patients for nearly eight years.

He returned to Big Bay only once, for the funeral of his dear friend, Norma Bouvier (Chief), a nurse he admired greatly and respected. After the funeral, Stanley gave Doctor Blue a tour of the new critical care and emergency rooms. The old timers watched as the two passed by, and the new employees too, with the look of people observing the ghost of a legend.

Nine years after they had left Big Bay, Rita died in Cuba of metastatic breast cancer. Doctor Blue took the small boat he and Rita used almost nightly to watch the sunset, and three miles off the shore he sprinkled Rita's ashes while the sun went down. In the darkness, he sat in the bobbing boat and wept until sunrise.

Most evenings, if the weather allowed, Doctor Blue climbed into the open bow twenty-one-foot aluminum fishing boat, pulled the rope to start the old Johnson outboard motor and traveled to Rita's spot. He would discuss the day with Rita, talking aloud so the dolphins that always greeted him could hear.

The red sunset had nearly disappeared into the darkness when the long Scarab racing boat coasted next to Doctor Blue's little aluminum boat. They bumped gently before the doctor stood, swathed in bright light.

"Please climb aboard, doctor," shouted a gravelly voice with a South African accent from behind the bright light. The man reached down.

"Go to hell," Doctor Blue replied.

"Come aboard or we shoot you."

"Go ahead, I couldn't care less."

Two men leapt from the Scarab into Doctor Blue's little boat, which lurched to the port side, nearly capsizing. The smaller of the invaders hit Doctor Blue against the right side of his face with a blackjack. The three men struggled to keep the boats together, fighting the wave action pushing them apart, lifting A.W.'s limp body to the Scarab's deck, losing their grip once, and desperately retrieving him from the water with a gaff hook on the end of a ten-foot pole.

…for a brief instant, Rita held him tightly, wrapping his entire body with warm love while the matron of the dolphin pod repeatedly pushed away the gaff hook with her nose…

The South African kicked the unconscious doctor lying on the deck. And then all three men laughed, pushing away the little aluminum boat.

"Should we sink it?" the short little man that had hit A.W. asked, machine gun in hand.

"No," said the third man, "Let it drift to the shore…look like a suicide." And he turned the spotlight off.

The short man took the helm. He pointed the Scarab in the direction of St. Kitts.

Doctor Blue awakened briefly in the forward hold, bouncing when the boat hit the big Atlantic waves in the darkness. The black hood that covered his head smelled of chloroform, and he gagged with nausea.

The second time he woke up, A.W. looked up at a gray concrete ceiling, tied spread-eagle on a metal bed, each ankle and wrist secured to the rusty bed frame by tight leather straps. A bottle of normal saline hung from a wheeled IV pole next to the bed. Doctor Blue followed the IV tubing down to his left forearm.

Drip…drip…drip… He felt a warm euphoric itchiness, watching a man in a white lab coat wearing wire rimmed glasses push the contents of a glass syringe into the IV tubing.

"That makes me happy, amigo," A.W. said in Spanish.

"A very special recipe just for you, doctor: meperidine hydrochloride, heroin, and cocaine. You will be addicted soon, amigo."

"Why are you doing this?"

"We have need of your services, doctor. This is our insurance you will never leave."

Doctor Blue closed his eyes and listened to the children playing games outside. He smiled a euphoric smile, watching red and blue butterflies land on Rita's bare breasts.

After thirty days of "treatments," the man with the wire rimmed glasses announced, "Soon you will meet the committee."

"What committee?"

"The committee which will explain your duties…doctor."

CHAPTER 2

EXPENSIVE STILETTOS

Seven thirty a.m., precisely.

At 7:30 a.m., she exited the pale brick Big Bay Hotel through its historic revolving front door, slipped into her green Volvo and navigated through the lingering morning fog to her destination, a cul-de-sac just past the McMillen residence. She knew the way now – up the steep hill to the west – fog drifting from the bay; she'd made this trek for six consecutive days.

From her spot behind a big sycamore tree, she observed the McMillen daily rituals: Mrs. McMillen putting things in the mailbox; then she and her daughter driving down the steep hill from their condo perched high above the city.

…that view from their condo must be amazing…

Then every morning a few minutes after his wife and daughter leave, Stanley stepping out onto the front porch wearing his black bathrobe and bending over to scoop up the morning edition of the *Big Bay Recorder.*

…must be nice to have a leisurely morning…

Then she would drive back to town, and walk through the business district, making inquiries and calling on the various doctors' offices.

Timothy added chili powder, roasted garlic, cumin, and two shakes of dark cocoa (his secret ingredient) to the crockpot mixture and was reaching for Hungarian paprika when she strolled through Poor Joe's front door. Pete, Doug, and Wayne leaned back in their chairs from the round table in the southwest corner, watching the blond lady with Brighton sunglasses approach.

Click…clack…click…and an irritating scraping sound when her left foot slipped on a wet spot and she almost fell, her expensive stilettos tapping on the hard oak floors with each step.

Machete turned his face away from her direction, listening to her clicking sounds moving closer to his left ear. His seeing eye dog, Little Miss, stood, her golden tail wagging back and forth, slowly at first, then not at all.

"Good morning." Timothy watched her approach, wiping his hand on a bar towel. "Lunch starts at noon."

From the top of the stairs, Wendell's eyes stared at the expensive stilettos and then traveled up to the owner of the shoes. *She's made for those shoes,* Wendell thought, allowing his eyes to settle on her breasts.

"Coffee sounds good." The lady smiled. She briefly stared at Timothy's amputated right arm, ending at the elbow, then glanced at her reflection in the mirror behind the bar.

"You look familiar." Timothy reached for the coffee pot.

"I'm a drug rep for Oleson Pharmaceuticals." She sat on a bar stool, again looking at herself in the Goebel Beer mirror, fixing her hair a little, before turning toward the men watching her from the southwest table. "And, I write articles for magazines."

"A freelancer?" Pete queried.

"That's correct! What's your name?"

"Pete."

"That's right, I write in the evenings when I travel. Keeps me from being bored and out of trouble." She added one creamer and two teaspoons of cane sugar to the cup.

"You have a name?" Wendell walked down the stairs from his room on the second floor.

She glanced toward the squeaking wooden steps and pushed the sunglasses up into her blond hair.

"Amy Hamilton. I'm a freelance journalist, working on a story about life in a small town like Big Bay."

Machete laughed. He looked in the direction of Amy with both blind eyes. "Lady, that would be a long novel."

Pete and Wayne laughed a little. Wendell did not. Doug stared.

"Jenifer down at the Cuban diner told me Timothy owned this place and that I would recognize him by his right arm," Amy said. "She told me there is a good story there."

Timothy simply stared at her.

"She told me that Stanley McMillen saved your life."

"You're a pharmaceutical rep; you know Stanley?" Timothy asked.

"You could say that, Tim. May I call you Tim? I've met Stan when I make hospital calls. I brought the nurses in the CCU lunch last month, and he stopped in to thank me."

"He's our close friend," Wendell spoke emphatically, standing. "And, he's a private man, we all are, and not fond of publicity either."

"Tell me this," she continued. "I heard that Stanley almost died last year. That true?"

"Yes," was the answer in unison.

"He was hit by a car," Machete said from his chair. "A very evil man tried to kill him."

"Well, that sounds like another great story. I hope we can talk more sometime. I've got appointments to keep. Thanks for the coffee. I'll be on my way." She reached into her purse and dropped a twenty on the bar.

Timothy pushed it back toward her. "On the house."

"Well, thank you, Tim! I'll make it a point to bring clients here when I'm in town."

"You'll have to tell me sometime how you hurt your hand." She stopped next to Wendell, reaching down and touching his disfigured right hand which rested on the table next to his coffee cup. With the fingertips of her left hand, one finger at a time in a rhythmic pattern, she caressed his mutated hand.

...damn she's beautiful...

"He caught a grenade in Vietnam and saved Timothy's life," Doug said. He turned his back and walked towards the coffee pot.

Amy pulled the sunglasses down on her face, walking away, leaving the twenty on the bar.

She drove east on Union Street and left to the Radio Shack store. She purchased a cell phone and spent the remainder of the day, far into the evening, texting messages back and forth between her cell phone and the new one. She messaged between the cell phones every day, no matter her location.

CHAPTER 3

THE COMPANY

The man wearing the wire rimmed glasses steadied Doctor Blue, who staggered as he shuffled into the plush board room. Sitting at a long polished mahogany table were three men on either side and a bearded man at the end, dressed in white suits.

A large horizontal paddle ceiling fan turned slowly, making sharp squeak…squeaking sounds during one phase of each revolution while the big blades reached downward, moving the sticky air.

The man pushed Doctor Blue's shoulders downward, forcing him to sit at the end, opposite the bearded man.

"Doctor Blue, this is the committee I spoke of. Please meet Ivan from Russia, Raul from Mexico, John from England, Hector from Brazil, Simon from South Africa, Jimmy from China, and at the end, Robert from the United States."

Doctor Blue shrugged. "So?"

"These are the men controlling your world, doctor. For your information, they control the entire world."

"Right."

A.W. Blue's eyes moved from face to face, staring at the brown eyes and blue eyes looking toward him. He went back to the icy blue eyes of the bearded man sitting at the other end.

"I have met you, Robert. Sixteen years ago you spoke at a medical convention in New Orleans. You spoke about the future of drugs in medicine." Doctor Blue paused, collecting his foggy memories. "You were the CEO of a pharmaceutical company."

"Very good, doctor," the bearded man replied.

"Quite a future," Doctor Blue replied sarcastically.

The man from South Africa said, "We are all businessmen and you are our doctor. Thank you for coming."

"I was kidnapped."

"Yes, that is true, and now you are a drug-addicted physician who will be quite willing to help us with our business. Unfortunately, your predecessor did not fare well and has died."

"What business?"

"The business that makes the world go around, doctor."

"What?"

"Sex, doctor. Sex is what makes the world go around. We provide young ladies to meet the worlds' desires – quality ladies from all over the world. You will run our health clinic to assure our ladies are in good health."

"I will not."

"Oh, you will, doctor, I assure you," Robert from the end of the table replied. "You know very well the withdrawal from the narcotic concoction you receive will cause an agonizing death. You, doctor, are going to be quite happy, checking our ladies for diseases and providing treatment before our orders are filled."

The man from China interjected, "We have a world-class clinic here, doctor."

"Coven Pharmaceuticals," Doctor Blue said, pointing to the other end of the table. "You were the CEO of Coven Pharmaceuticals."

The bearded man smiled. "Still am, doctor."

●●●

Doctor A.W. Blue worked in the women's clinic located at the intersection of Fort and Prince streets in the city of Basseterre on the island of St. Kitts. Each evening, the man with the wire rimmed glasses injected the opiate cocktail through an IV port. Each night

Doctor Blue would drift to sleep, dreaming of Rita and feeling the warmth of her love covering him entirely.

The aluminum fishing boat eventually washed up and flipped over on the northern Cuba beach. The Cuban Navy had searched for him as did Quinn O'Malley and the True Believers, using their stealth helicopters. Finally, A.W. Blue was declared missing at sea, and Quinn called Stanley in Big Bay with the sad news.

Doctor Blue performed physicals on the many young ladies brought to the island for the purposes of human trafficking by the group simply known as *The Company*.

CHAPTER 4

FOR OLD TIMES' SAKE

Stanley walked into his office located next to the Cardiac Care Unit, following the Friday morning patient report. His secretary called.

"The drug rep from Oleson Pharmaceuticals is here to see you."

Stanley glanced at the wall clock and his daily planner.

"Tell her I have only a few minutes." He opened the door and stepped out.

"Hi, Stan!"

Amy Hamilton walked quickly towards him, her shoes click-clacking on the tile. She hugged Stanley tightly in full view of the CCU staff. "I have just one little request."

She followed him back into his office. Amy closed the door.

"What's up, Amy?"

"Oleson Pharmaceuticals has purchased Coven Pharmaceuticals. We now have oxycodone and Tylenol with codeine, all three strengths, and Demerol."

Stanley shrugged. "That's nice, I guess. Why you telling me? We get our cardiac meds from you and I think the hospital gets its narcotics from Horizon."

"I'm hoping you'll influence the head of pharmacy to sign a contract with us. I know you two are friends."

"Not sure that's appropriate, Amy."

"Just hoping you'd help me…behind on my quota this quarter." She paused. "For old times' sake, Stan…please?"

"We were teenagers, Amy."

"Would have been more if my parents hadn't moved to New York."

She moved closer, pressing her right breast against him.

"Guess we'll never know. I'll mention it to him next week."

"Thanks!"

As they exited the office, Amy turned and hugged Stanley again.

"Thank you, Stanley." And she waved at the nurses watching from behind the nurses' station.

CHAPTER 5

A VERY BAD PLACE

Richard Elmore Fortin could not understand Belvia Chase's screaming voice on the telephone.

"Belvia…Belvia…Belvia…BELVIA…STOP!"

Silence except for gasps.

"What's wrong?"

"Norah is missing."

Richard glanced at his watch.

"How long?"

"She only had a half-day of school and then a babysitting job until Mrs. Hilson got home from parent-teachers conference at 5:00."

Shit, four hours, Richard thought.

"Mrs. Hilson never went to her appointment cuz she said Norah never showed up."

…eight hours…

"How old is Norah?"

"Fourteen; just started the ninth grade."

"She have a boyfriend?"

"No."

"You sure?"

"No."

"I'm in Havana with Quinn. We'll be back in an hour. Call the police."

•••

Norah Chase loved living in Key West. Compared to Anchorage and that life of turmoil, Key West seemed like a dream. Besides, her body had changed, and Justin in the band smiled at her a lot.

The Bahama Village Band had been invited to march in the annual Key West Christmas parade, and she had practiced each song on her tenor sax for weeks. Tomorrow evening the parade started at White and Truman, then down Duval.

...I'm so excited I could bust...marching right next to Justin...

She had passed Fausto's Grocery Store and crossed White Street at the National Weather Service office with the Glynn Archer School in sight when a young man driving a black Ford pulled up next to her with the passenger window down and shouted, "Your little brother was hit by a car. Your mom wants you to meet her in the emergency room. Get in, hurry." And he flashed a badge. He pushed open the passenger door.

Norah climbed in with her backpack and fastened the seat belt. The car sped down White Street. As it turned left at the next intersection, a large black hand reached around the headrest, covering her face with a chloroform-soaked rag, clamped tight.

...Mommy...Mommy...Mommy...

She awakened briefly and struggled in the back seat of the small airplane. The large black man sitting beside her stuck a needle through her dress into her thigh, injecting the contents from a glass syringe.

All black.

Just briefly she awakened a second time, bouncing. Powerful engines roared next to her. The cotton bag over her head smelled sweet – a pungent smell burning her throat with each breath.

All black, again.

Doctor Blue sat next to the teenager lying on the clinic cot, taking her pulse, watching her eyelids flutter while she regained consciousness. Her clothing had been cut away, except for pink panties and her bra. He counted six injection sites in her left anterior thigh and shook his head. Two of the injection sites had developed large hematomas. He also noted a contusion over her left eye.

…well, she's a scrapper…

Mental notes, nothing ever written or recorded in any way.

"How old are you?" he asked when she opened both eyes and stared up at him.

"Where am I?"

"In a clinic. I am the doctor."

"Where's my mom? Is my brother Steve going to be OK?"

Doctor Blue patted her hand. "You are in a special clinic. Let's get you better first. How old are you?"

"Fourteen. Where's my mom?"

"What's your name, dear? I need a name."

"Norah Chase…WHERE'S MY MOM?"

Doctor Blue took a deep breath.

Norah sat up on the cot.

"What's your address?" he asked.

"817 White Street."

"Key West?"

"Yes, of course Key West. Our friend Richard rents it to us. Where am I?"

"Far away from Key West, I'm afraid."

Norah stared at the old man.

"We are in a very evil place, Norah. And right now we are in great danger. Say nothing to anyone, except me. Just know that we are in great danger if you do."

"What's this place?"

"This is a bad place."

…Mommy…

"Help me…"

I will find a way, the old doctor thought. I can't even help myself. He looked out the window, shaking his head back and forth.

•••

"What were you whispering to the new girl?" Wire-Rim inquired, injecting the evening drug cocktail. "We reviewed the video. You were told no whispering."

"She's a frightened little girl. I was calming her."

"No whispering. Understood?"

"Yes."

"Is she a virgin?"

"Yes."

"Good. The prince desires only virgins."

CHAPTER 6

ONE MICROCHIP

The Key West City Police discovered nothing. Their usual sources, eager for favor or drinking money, had seen nothing. No rumors. Even at Glynn Archer School the inquiries came up short.

Richard stayed with Belvia and her two children, trying to reassure without confidence in his own efforts.

The Monday morning following the Christmas parade, Quinn O'Malley and the Key West chief of police drove to 817 White Street in an unmarked car. Quinn, Richard, Chief Harlan, and Belvia sat around a picnic table in the backyard, surrounded by a white fence.

"The Cuban Intelligence Agency told me yesterday that they have an ongoing investigation regarding the disappearances of young ladies from the Caribbean. Several have resurfaced months later in Europe, China, Saudi Arabia, and the U.S. The Cubans recently had an agent go undercover, posing as a tenth grader in an affluent area of Mexico City where three girls had disappeared the previous year."

Belvia trembled. Richard hugged her.

"She was kidnapped five months ago," Quinn continued. "The Cubans were able to track her to Martinique, following a chip they had implanted in her breast."

"No…no…no," Belvia whispered to Richard.

Quinn paused long enough to light a Cuban cigar.

"You trust the intel?" the chief inquired.

"No reason not to."

"Friday afternoon a plane registered to a dummy company flew from Key West to Martinique's Aimé Césaire International Airport. Putting this puzzle together, Norah may be on Martinique.

"Oh…my baby…please…"

"Let's go," Richard said.

"The Cubans have been watching a large building on Martinique since their agent disappeared. They believe this is a big operation, international – human trafficking, drugs, and shadow power brokers."

Belvia Chase slumped into Richard's arms, muttering, "Sons of bitches."

"I'm going to find Norah," he whispered to the head on his chest, "and then I'm going to kill the sons of bitches."

Quinn reached over and touched Belvia.

"The Cuban Special Forces have been planning an attack for the past week, waiting for a moonless night which is next Tuesday. Their general is delighted that the True Believers will be joining them. We meet tomorrow at San Antonio de los Baños Airfield, at midnight."

Quinn looked at Belvia.

"Fidel hates drugs and human trafficking."

He lit a fresh cigar.

"So do I."

● ● ●

The True Believers and Cuban Special Forces gathered in Cuba's military airport – eighteen True Believers and twenty Cuban Special Forces – watching the Cuban two-star general spread a large map on a green metal table.

"We have been watching a building…here," he said in Spanish, pointing with a slender stick to the intersection of Rue Martin Luther King and Rue de la Liberation in the City of Fort De France.

"The last signal from our agent came from this vicinity. We have since observed nefarious activity coming through the gates of this compound – trucks entering and leaving, mostly at night. Many teenagers have been spotted inside the compound on aerial photos. Also, there are armed men there. As best we can count, again from aerial photographs, about thirty."

He looked at the assembly, lit a cigar and continued.

"We are honored that you and the True Believers have joined us, General O'Malley. President Castro sends his best wishes and would like to see you upon our return. I understand a young lady, a friend of Richard's, is missing and may well be at this building."

He nodded in Richard's direction.

"There is a main gate and also smaller doors on each of the other three walls," he continued in Spanish. "We have observed that a truck leaves the compound every night at 0230. Our Special Forces will storm the entrance when the gate is opened for the truck. Copter number one will land inside the compound next to this large building where we believe the young women are being held. Copter two will circle, providing air support and gun cover. Copter three will land to the west…here, with six men going through this small door and six through the west door."

The general relit his cigar and puffed it twice.

"We should have the compound secure in ten minutes, maximum. Then we will let the Martinique government know we have arrived and expect help…or not."

He smiled.

CHAPTER 7

GET 'ER DONE, SON

"Think you'll be late tonight?" Danielle asked, watching Stanley slip into his white lab coat.

"Hope not; have you seen my pager and car keys?"

"You left them on the dining room table."

"Thanks. Why?"

"I thought maybe we'd catch an early movie and get a bite to eat after."

"Sounds good to me. I've got to finish some reports for tomorrow's department head meeting. Give you a call when I'm finished. What're your plans?"

"Going shopping for Chloe. We looked for summer dresses and new outfits last Saturday, and I'm going to surprise her. She's growing like a weed, almost as tall as I am!"

"That's what happens when you're closing in on sixteen. She's as beautiful as her mom." Stanley hugged Danielle. "I wouldn't want to go through those years again for anything."

"She's a good girl, Stan."

"I know. Just saying."

●●●

His office chair felt uncomfortable, even though he had a special padded one...*if I had to do this crap every day, I'd quit...*

Stanley rechecked the census data for November and recalculated the expense report for the third time, adding several receipts he had forgotten about in his bottom drawer.

The phone rang.

"Hi, Stan; Amy here. Guess it's my lucky day, catching you in your office. Would you be a dear and meet me in the hotel lobby for just a few. I have to leave in fifteen minutes, but have one more thing to share. It's kinda important."

"I'll walk right over; fresh air will clear my brain."

Amy sat on the rose-colored loveseat in the corner of the hotel lobby, alone. She stood when Stanley approached, dragging a chair with him, hugging him before he sat down.

"I talked to the pharmacy director at Big Bay General on the phone this morning. He doesn't know anything about Oleson taking over Coven…nothing about our expanded inventory. He said, when I asked him, that you never mentioned a word."

"I'm planning on mentioning it tomorrow at the department head meeting."

"Well, Stanley, I already brought it up, and he told me that the hospital has a contract with Horizon Pharmaceuticals for all narcotics. He's not interested."

"Sorry."

"I'm depending on you Stanley; you know the people that can change this."

"Come on, Amy, what the hell. Don't be so impatient."

"There's more to the story, Stan, than I've shared with you."

"Well?"

"The vacant building next to Radio Shack is going to be remodeled and turned into a pain clinic."

Stanley looked at Amy.

"A subsidiary of Oleson Pharmaceuticals will be sending a physician and staff to run it."

"Don't do this, Amy."

"Why not?"

"This just doesn't smell right. The company you're working for opening a pain clinic after purchasing a company that specializes in narcotics and putting pressure on you to have the narcotics funneled through Big Bay General? At least it has the appearance of something beneath you. Let me help. I know lots of people: here, in the Keys, in Marathon, Key West…Come on, Amy. You know what I'm saying."

Amy looked away, just briefly, then at the floor while reaching into her purse. She then looked up, holding the Radio Shack phone.

"Stan, this transaction must take place."

Amy pushed a button, activating the phone. "And, I need your promise to support this at every opportunity, starting with tomorrow's meeting. People trust you. They will listen to you."

"Kinda sounds like a threat, Amy…or what?"

Amy scrolled up the phone's text messages, reading them out loud in a whisper while tapping the screen with her manicured finger nail.

"This phone was purchased by Stanley James McMillen," she said in a chilling tone. "I've been paying your phone bill, honey. Oh, look at last night's message you sent me."

Stanley leaned close to the phone being held tightly in Amy's left hand. The message read:

"Yesterday brought back the feelings from high school, the warm closeness. I can't wait to be with you again."

"Why are you doing this? We loved each other. I don't understand…we loved each other, Amy."

…the Chevy's windows were steamed. Together they rolled Amy's white winter coat with a fur collar into a back-seat pillow…

"What the hell, Amy! I want to help. Give me the damn phone!"

"You're kidding, right?" she retorted.

Stanley's arms grew goosebumps, hearing the chill in her voice.

"We were just a couple of kids having fun. Give me a break… in love."

She tapped on the phone repeatedly.

"We've been sexting for quite a spell, Stan. I suspect Mrs. McMillen will be disappointed, to say the least. Oh, the scandal for the Big Bay gossips. And the nurses that worship you, oh…so disappointed."

Stanley reached for the phone.

His chest ached.

"Give it to me, Amy."

"Nope. If you come closer, I'll scream. Now you take care of business and help me and this phone goes into a shredder. Otherwise, your guess who sees it next. People've been seeing us hug for the last several months, HONEY."

Stanley stared with absolute anger.

…shit, that's what I get for being a hugger…

Without another word, he walked through the historic revolving hotel door and back to his office, his mind numb and racing.

Amy Hamilton smirked while pulling her suitcase toward the green Volvo.

…you ain't seen nothin' yet, Stanley McMillen…

Driving on the Seven Hills Highway leaving Big Bay, she phoned Chicago.

"Vladimir! Things are on track in Big Bay. Contract will be approved tomorrow."

"Good job, Amy. You amaze me each time. Now I understand the reason Robert made you a boss, eleven clinics now."

"This one is the most difficult," she replied.

●●●

Wyatt Tiffany's presence filled any room. A tall, big man, his bodacious personality matched his size and his ego. As Big Bay General's new administrator, he loved to impress the board of directors and staff with his political connections, frequently calling senators, congressmen, and governors by their first names.

Stanley sat exhausted at the table.

Danielle could tell something was wrong when Stanley came home last evening. She watched her husband walk around the condo with a distracted look in his eyes, not finishing sentences, and not listening when she asked questions. Chloe noticed, too. Winking at Danielle, she said, "Mom bought me a wedding dress today, I'm going to get married, Daddy." To which he replied, "That's nice, honey." Danielle postponed the evening out. Stanley said, "thank you" and hugged her tighter than usual.

Stanley did not sleep much the night before the important meeting. When he did fall asleep, about 4:00 a.m., he dreamed…

…where's the time clock…damn Tiffany installed a time clock. Even the docs have to punch in…it's not here…in this a new hallway… they've moved the cafeteria…turkey roll and beef pot pies…come to this… turkey roll…where the hell's the time clock…here's a new door…the power plant…coal ash…damn deep coal ash…ruining my shoes and pants…here's the way out…crawl under the semi…I can't get out, there's a fence down here…I'm trapped…

The hospital department head meeting started at 9:00 a.m. Administrator Tiffany sat at the head of the table, smiling his big Dallas smile.

All he needs is a cowboy hat, Director of Nurses, Ramona, thought, sitting next to the big man. She made a mental note that Stanley looked awful.

"Got a call yesterday from my buddy Bill, head of the Senate Committee on Veterans' Affairs in D.C.," Wyatt Tiffany said, starting the meeting. "Says a friend of his is setting up pain clinics around the country and plans on opening one right here in Big Bay, down on Union Street. This friend has interest in a pharmaceutical company that will give us a break on pain medications, and we would help this little company a great deal by providing these medications to the clinic, simply here to help the poor unfortunates suffering after serving our beloved country and the other folks in our community needlessly suffering as well. My friend assures me our little clinic will have the Veterans Administration approval, since the nearest VA clinic is far removed."

Stanley looked across the table at Jim, the director of pharmacy.

"That shouldn't be a problem, right, Jim?" Mr. Tiffany asked.

"We have a contract with Horizon Pharmaceuticals for all our narcotics and sedatives, Mr. Tiffany."

"I checked on that, young man. Why, it's not an exclusive contract in any way, just an agreement to provide. You go ahead and sign a contract with Oleson Pharmaceuticals. They'll save us a considerable amount over time, and since the pharmaceutical companies are not allowed by law to open retail outlets, we'll be helping this fledgling clinic get started. A win-win, I say. Get 'er done, son."

"Yes, sir."

"Shouldn't we ask Horizon if they would be willing to match Oleson's pricing?" Stanley asked.

Wyatt Tiffany's big smile froze, for just an instant.

"Why, Stanley, better to have two hogs at the trough. Jim, give Oleson a call."

"I have no idea what that means, Mr. Tiffany. You're the boss… your decision."

"You got that right, son."

●●●

Danielle inquired, that evening, how the department head meeting went.

"I don't remember, honey."

Then he turned and looked at his wife in a way she had never seen in the eighteen years she had known him.

"Not so good, Danielle."

Danielle gripped Stanley's shirt and pulled her husband close.

"You and I have been special, almost reading each other's

minds, since I walked into that CCU eighteen years ago. We feel each other's feelings. When your heart feels heavy, I know, and right now it feels like a stone, like you have a heavy load. I love you. I am your loudest cheerleader and closest friend. I'm in this fight, by your side, Stanley James McMillen. I'm right here," she punched her forefinger into his chest over his heart, "and I'm going to be at your side forever, helping you through whatever the hell is wrong, just like you've helped me, side by side, no matter what...." Her voice faded into a whisper. She sucked in a deep breath.

Chloe watched and listened.

"And besides, Stanley. You don't need this damn job. We could leave for Key West tomorrow."

CHAPTER 8

THE DEBACLE

Perfectly timed.

The heavy, reinforced wrought iron gate opened for the Chevrolet truck, and Cuban Special Forces trotted through the opening. The men flattened the truck tires, blocking the gate, just as the first helicopter flew up over the marina and flooded the compound with brilliant light. Armed men, streaming from their barracks, threw their weapons to the ground and their arms in the air after the first burst from the helicopter's Gatling gun.

Richard Elmore Fortin was the first to come off the second helicopter which landed next to the large two-story dormitory style building, and the first through the front door to see hundreds of youngsters, boys and girls, sitting at individual tables, making cigars. They screamed, watching the soldiers charge into their large room.

A child sat at each small table, which had a stack of tobacco leaves on the left, a pot of glue, a box of cigar bands, and a chaveta to trim the cigars. The children scattered past the startled Special Forces, running outside.

The Cuban general yanked opened the rear doors of an old truck and stared at cases of cigars labeled, COHIBA La HABANA, CUBA. He opened a box, bit the end from a cigar, and lit it.

"Cigarros falsificado!" he shouted, pointing to the truck's contents. He handed a cigar to O'Malley then took a second puff.

"Sabor a mierda," (flavor like shit) the general said, flinging the cigar against the brick wall.

Richard walked through the swirling children toward a gray windowless door on the far wall and opened it. A man wearing a dirty New York Yankees baseball cap rapidly fed pages, ripping them from a ledger, into a shredder. Richard walked quickly toward the man, his hands up, shouting in Spanish, "I just want to talk."

The man picked up a pistol from the desk and shot Richard in the chest.

Richard continued to walk toward the startled man, now twenty feet away.

"You cannot kill me. I am a spirit. I just want to talk."

…damn, that hurt. Glad O'Malley made me wear a vest…

The man shot Richard in the chest again. He was aiming at Richard's head when Richard drew his revolver and shot the man once, between the eyes.

Richard looked down at the ledger, titled *St. Kitts.* There were columns labeled Date, Country of Origin, Age, Tag Number, Gallons used. Half the ledger had been shredded. He folded the leather bound ledger and slipped it under the bulletproof vest.

Then he reached to the floor, picked up the dirty Yankees cap, and put it on.

The Martinique police and local authorities arrived, exclaiming their gratitude for the help in uncovering such an evil sweatshop. The mayor promised the children would be cared for and the armed men punished. The chief of police nodded his head in agreement.

The disheartened Cuban Special Forces left on their helicopters.

Quinn O'Malley placed his arm on Richard's shoulder while they walked down Rue de la Liberation in the direction of their helicopter.

"You OK? Couple of holes in your shirt."

"Thanks for the vest."

"Welcome."

"That is what we call a debacle, Richard; and now you know why we don't share everything with the Cuban military."

"I have a ledger under my vest. Must be important; the guy was shredding it."

"Nice hat."

"Norah," Richard said.

"I know. This is going to be hard, telling her mom. We are going to find her."

"Yes, we are," Richard replied, rubbing at the hole in his shirt closest to his heart.

"There's a microchip detector on the desk, next to the paper shredder."

"Dammit," Quinn said.

Chapter 9

Erin Kerr's Mom

Wednesday morning, the day following the department head meeting, and Stanley simply could not tolerate the thought of seeing Wyatt Tiffany strutting about, making his morning "rounds."

"I just called Ramona and told her I'm going fishing and not to expect to see me today." Stanley walked into the kitchen wearing jeans and a heavy wool shirt. "Wendell told me yesterday the perch are biting just off the power plant."

"Stan, the bay only froze over five days ago."

"Wendell said it's fine."

"Wendell fell through the ice and almost drowned right before I moved to town, Stan."

"That he did, honey. Hasn't happened since. I need to go fishing, Wendell has the gear and said the ice is safe. See you tonight... with dinner."

Stanley kissed Danielle, hugged Chloe, and walked to the garage.

"Mom, Dad doesn't fish. He's never gone fishing."

"I know, honey. He just needs time away from the hospital to think."

"Mom...?"

"Yes."

"You know Erin Kerr's mom?"

"Yup, Mary, she works in admitting, why?"

"Erin overheard her mom on the telephone telling someone that dad is having an affair with a drug company lady."

"What did you say to Erin?"

"I said 'no way.' No way, Mom."

"Let's go in the living room, honey. You're going to be late for school."

Sitting on the couch, next to her mother, Chloe had never, ever, seen the fiery expression, swirling with a soft glow, coming from her hazel eyes.

Danielle held her daughter's hand.

"It's easier to tear other people down than it is to build yourself up. That's what the insecure people do. They gossip and demean and by doing so, think they are somehow superior. If they really and truly cared, they would not say a word. Do you understand?"

"Yes, Mom. But, aren't you worried?"

"To be honest, I am. Your dad and I have been together for eighteen years. I have never seen him this upset."

Chloe watched her mother's face.

"Ramona told me about the rumors circulating, last Friday. She doesn't believe them for a second."

Danielle paused. Chloe watched Danielle twist her wedding ring around and around.

"I know it's not true, Chloe. There's something bad happening, but I know that is not true."

"Why doesn't he say?"

"He's trying to protect the people he loves. That I have seen, many times. He becomes quiet until the problem is fixed. It's what he does, Chloe. He becomes angry inside; then when it looks like everything is about to fall apart, he emerges like the hero he really is. Your daddy really is a hero, you know. And, I will tell you this, I don't give a damn what is happening, honey; your daddy and I told each other 'For better or worse,' holding hands on Quinn O'Malley's boat off the shore of Cuba…I meant it."

Chloe snuggled close to her mother.

"I hope I can be this strong when I'm a grown-up."

"There is not a question in my mind, Chloe."

"I'm going to skip school today."

•••

"Here, tie this rope around you," Wendell said. He tied the other end around his waist.

"I've never been ice fishing." Stanley took his gloves off and tied a slip knot. "Is this usual procedure?"

"Nope," Wendell replied. "Just a little insurance, 'case we hit a weak spot."

Stanley smiled.

They sat on three-legged stools, Wendell's specially equipped sleigh between them, furnished with bait, extra equipment, filament line, bobbers, and Schlitz beer in longneck bottles, watching for movement of their little bobbers in the ice holes.

"Hope you like olive loaf and sliced onion with mustard on pumpernickel."

"Sounds delicious."

"Brought chips, too."

They fished silently for almost twenty minutes. Wendell caught fourteen perch and two rock bass. Stanley caught seven perch and a bluegill.

Wendell pulled a fifteenth perch through the hole and asked, "You want to talk about it?"

Stanley looked at Wendell's eyes, peeking through the ski mask. "I'm being blackmailed."

"Figured something like that," the old vet growled.

"What?" Stanley exclaimed.

"Couple of drunks – guess there were three of them – their wives work at the hospital – were yucking it up at Poor Joe's Saturday night, saying all sorts of shit like you're having an affair with that drug rep, sneaking off to see her at the hotel, stuff like that."

Stanley watched his fishing bobber disappear repeatedly under the water and resurface.

"You gonna pull that one in?"

Stanley turned the reel, his mind spinning.

"The guys listened for a few minutes. Machete got up from our table first. He bent down and whispered something to Little Miss and undid her leash. He walked over to those three guys like he could see. Wayne and I followed. Timothy and Pete came over from the popcorn machine and we surrounded them."

Wendell blew his nose.

"'What YOU gonna do?' the big fat one said, and he gave Machete a push.

"That's a mistake," Stanley said, removing the hook from a largemouth bass.

"Nice fish. Fillet that one; I'll show you how. Yup, bad mistake. The fat fellow stood up just in time for Little Miss to secure his private parts in her mouth and give them a twist. Down he went, hollering that he was going to call the police. Then the guy named Randy pulled a pistol and pointed it at Little Miss. He put it down when Timothy reached under the counter and got his revolver."

"Holy shit!" Stanley said while rebaiting the hook.

"Stanley is not having an affair," Machete told those three. They were all scared and shaky. He told 'em to go tell their wives he's having no affair and if hears them say it again, he'd have some of his friends explain it to them more clearly."

"I love that little Mexican," Stanley said.

"Then Timothy said to them, 'You guys, as far as I'm concerned, this never happened.' He told them that if they lodged a complaint, none of us saw a thing and then he told that guy Art that it was up to him to explain to the Mrs. how he got the bruises down there."

Stanley shook his head and smiled.

"Want a sandwich and a beer?" Wendell asked.

"Yup."

"So, what's going on?"

"Amy Hamilton was my girlfriend in high school. She left during our senior year when her father took a job in New York. Never saw her again till she showed up this fall, working as a sales rep for Oleson Pharmaceuticals."

"She's a beauty, Stan."

"That she is, and she knows it, Wendell."

"So what's going on?"

"Oleson Pharmaceuticals just took over Coven Pharmaceuticals, a major provider of opiates and narcotics to hospitals. Amy wants the contract for narcotics at Big Bay General taken away from Horizon Pharmaceuticals and given to her. And, between you and me, her company is opening a pain clinic just down the street from Poor Joe's, next to Radio Shack. They want our hospital to be the provider of narcotics to the clinic. Oleson Pharmaceuticals is based in Chicago. I think this is drug laundering. Anyway, when I objected and offered to help her find another job, she pulled out a phone she'd purchased in my name and showed all the sex messages I'd sent her the past few months. She threatened to give it to Danielle and spread it all around, unless I helped her secure the contract."

Wendell put his fishing pole on the ice.

"Have you told Danielle?

"Not yet."

"She's your best friend, Stan."

"Yup."

"We need to get the guys together; call O'Malley and Fortin?"

"Not yet."

•••

"I've got dinner!" Stanley said, walking into the kitchen with a bucket of fish. "All cleaned and ready to fry."

He looked at Danielle and Chloe, standing side by side, holding hands.

...oh shit...

"Come talk to us, Daddy."

CHAPTER 10

NICE HAT

Quinn O'Malley phoned his wife while riding in the helicopter back to Cuba from Martinique.

"I really need you to be with us when Richard and I tell Belvia we didn't find her daughter. Would you meet us at the marina? We'll be landing in Havana in ninety minutes."

"What happened Quinn?" Debra asked.

"Cuban intel wrong. It was a sweatshop, using child labor to make counterfeit Cuban cigars."

"I'm sorry."

"Me too, Deb. Mostly I'm really sorry our honeymoon has been messed up."

"Quinn O'Malley, we've been honeymooning from the day we met in Anchorage. And, old man, I look forward to a long, long honeymoon with you. I'm so happy you said yes. Besides, we had a wonderful wedding, with Fidel signing the papers and Richard as your best man. Life goes on. We'll go through it better with each other."

"You're right."

"Of course I am. Never grow weary of saying that." And Debra laughed.

"Speaking of Richard, take a look at his new hat."

Debra stood next to their boat, *Key West Dreamer*, her hair blowing back, the key lime green dress flapping about. Quinn stared through the window at his wife coming closer and closer as the XS-1 stealth helicopter landed on the marina lawn.

Richard looked too and then said, "You're one fortunate man, Quinn."

"Yup."

She hugged her husband first and kissed him on the lips and his cheek. Then Debra looked at Richard staring at them. His face seemed older than last week, and the scar on his right cheek more pronounced. She felt sorry for him, for no particular reason.

"Nice hat, Richard." She hugged him.

"Thanks. I like it."

"Same color as your glass eye. Gonna scare the crap out of people."

"Good."

"Didn't know you're a Yankees fan."

"I'm not."

The trio had traveled 60 miles north when Richard took his shirt off and removed the bullet-proof vest. He handed the folded ledger to Debra.

"Ever see anything like this in your DEA days?"

The men watched Debra unfold the leather ledger and turn the remaining pages.

"Yes," she said after several minutes. "It's a shipping log. They are sending items to St. Kitts."

She paused and stared at the ledger for several seconds before continuing. Quinn slowed the engines to hear her better.

Debra spoke next in a soft, icy voice, trembling.

"See this heading…Tag Number…the sons of bitches are dealing in human trafficking. These are microchip identification numbers. They're sending girls from Martinique to St. Kitts."

Quinn reached and took his wife's hand.

"You sure?"

"Yes. Saw one just like this in Seattle. Human trafficking guys. They were human traffickers. What day did Norah go missing?"

"December 5th," Richard replied.

Debra turned the remaining pages. She stopped on the second-to-last page and read, "December…U.S.A.…age approx. 16…number 9a-783xx…163 gallons."

"Shit," Quinn muttered.

They looked at each other for what seemed like a very long time before Richard spoke. "Well, we are not going to tell Belvia."

"Quinn, send our plane to pick up Katie in Big Bay, and fly her to be with Belvia," said Debra. "I'm going with you guys…to St. Kitts."

…she called it our plane…God I love her…

Debra phoned Katie without waiting for a response.

Katie picked up the rectory phone in Big Bay.

"Hi Katie. Belvia's oldest daughter – you remember Norah – she's been kidnapped by some human traffickers. Quinn is sending a plane to get you, so you can be with Belvia in Key West."

"Oh my God," Katie whispered very softly. Debra could barely understand. "What time will the plane be here?"

Debra looked at Quinn and formed the word "when" with her lips. He held up three fingers.

"Quinn said at 3:00."

"I'll be ready. Would it be better to bring Belvia back to Big Bay?"

"We talked about that. Richard said there is no way Belvia would leave Key West with her daughter missing."

"And, Katie, she does not know that Norah was taken by human traffickers, only that she's missing."

"What can I say up here?"

"Tell everyone to pray as hard as they know how. Tell them that Norah is missing and to pray as hard as they can." Debra could feel Katie smile through the phone.

"I can do that," the Methodist preacher said, running her fingers through her red hair.

● ● ●

The doorbell rang. Belvia peeked through the curtain and opened the front door at 817 White Street. She cried immediately, seeing Richard, Quinn, and Debra standing on her front porch without her daughter.

Richard put both arms around her body, her sobbing face next to the holes in his shirt.

"We know where she is, Belvia."

"Why don't you have her?"

"Debra just figured it out from some new intel. We'll get her real soon."

She pushed back, just enough to see his face.

"Promise?"

"Promise!"

Debra touched Belvia's shoulder.

"Katie is flying down this afternoon to be with you while we go pick up your daughter."

"You guys must be some sort of angels," Belvia wiped her face on Richard's shirt. She noticed two holes in the shirt and explored with her forefinger the one over his heart.

Belvia inserted her forefinger into the bullet hole and pushed against his bruised rib. Richard winced and looked down at her eyes looking up at him with terror and love.

CHAPTER 11

EVEN IN THE AWFUL TIMES

Katie and Doug dropped their children off at school before driving to the airport.

"I can't imagine the terror in Belvia's soul right now," Katie said, "but mostly, the fear poor Norah is living."

"Me neither," Doug replied.

…they've got shotguns…damn…damn…the damn VC have shotguns…angels…love the smell of her long blond hair…

They stood outside in the cold watching the sleek white Gulfstream S-21 circle the Big Bay Airport once and then land.

"It's the only one in the world," Doug said, "and we get to ride in it – Mach 2."

"Even more amazing, Doug, is their love, the absolute love of our friends – never a question of if, only how they will help each other. We are so blessed, even during the awful times."

"I know."

● ● ●

"We heard the roar of O'Malley's plane. You know if he's here?" Pete asked when Doug walked into Poor Joe's for lunch.

"Yeah, nothing roars like O'Malley's plane," Wendell added.

"Nope, he's in Key West. Sent his plane to pick up Katie."

Machete stroked Little Miss's head.

"What's going on?" Pete asked.

Timothy listened from behind the bar.

"Debra called Katie this morning from Key West; said Belvia's oldest has been kidnapped."

"Sweet little Norah?" Pete exclaimed.

"Yup, Deb said she's fourteen now…has disappeared."

Machete stroked Little Miss harder.

"She wants us all to pray as hard as we know how. She said Quinn and Richard are gathering the True Believers and for us to pray as hard as we can."

Timothy poured fresh coffee in the various empty cups.

Little Miss licked Machete's hand.

Doctor McCaferty walked in. "Heard the roar of O'Malley's Gulfstream. What's going on?"

"Belvia Chase's oldest daughter has been kidnapped," Doug said. "Katie is flying down to be with Belvia while they find Norah."

"That poor family has been through hell," Doctor McCaferty said. "Norah is a sweet girl." His brown eyes became sad.

"O'Malley and his boys looking for her?"

"Will be soon," Doug replied.

"Good. That's who I'd want looking for me."

• • •

The three ladies hugged in the center of Belvia's living room. Debra, Katie, and Belvia surrounded themselves with each other's arms and silently embraced. Quinn, Richard and a True Believer named Mike, who had picked up Katie at the airport, looked on from the pool area through the open French doors.

Spontaneously, Katie began to whisper a prayer.

"Lord Jesus, our hearts are breaking right now. We do not understand why such evil is allowed in our lives. We trust you and know someday we will understand. Hold us close to you and give us the strength to trust you. Please be with Norah. Hold her close and send your angels to protect her and bring her home soon."

Then Debra turned and faced the men.

"Let's go get Norah."

CHAPTER 12

WHEN HOPE TURNS TO DUST

The True Believers gathered in the private hangar next to Key West International's main terminal. Eighteen men and a lone lady in the large galvanized metal Quonset hut were sitting on brown metal folding chairs. Quinn pointed to an enlarged aerial photo taped to the west wall.

"Richard just returned from Basseterre on St. Kitts. Turns out he makes a great street beggar, too," Quinn said, grinning. He turned on a laser pointer. "And, we've been gathering aerial intel for the past week as well: photos, ultrasonic, thermal, acoustic, and ultraviolet imaging."

"This is the compound, located at the intersection of Fort and Prince. The business is a sex cartel known only as *The Company*. We believe it to be a conglomerate with tentacles worldwide, reaching into medicine, banking, oil, drugs, real estate, and politics. As you can see, this is a formidable compound, walled with machine gun turrets located at all four corners. The walls are twenty feet tall and six feet thick. There is razor wire just over the inside ledge, out of sight from the street."

Richard stood. "There is only one entrance. It's a double gate with an atrium. A vehicle enters through the open gate which closes, the vehicle is inspected, and only then is the second gate opened. It would take a tank to get through those gates." He rubbed under his glass eye. "A big tank going fast."

Quinn moved the pointer to the next photo on the wall.

"This is where the girls are being held, built like a dormitory. We think they are downstairs. The second level is a medical clinic or hospital of some sort. The third story is *The Company's* executive offices and three condos used for entertaining guests."

He pointed the laser to a single story, flat-roofed building near the gate.

"The mercenaries are housed here. As best we can estimate from the time-lapse satellite photos, there are ninety soldiers total, likely working eight-hour shifts, with thirty on duty at a given time."

Quinn tossed the laser pointer on the table and walked over to Richard.

"We exist for this very moment," he said. "We know what to do."

He paused.

"And, we know better than anyone else how to do it."

"Team Cobra, go in first. Take out the machine gun turrets and circle with your light on."

"Team Mongoose, you land next to the dormitory on Team Cobra's all clear, and secure the girls. Richard, Deb, and I ride with you."

"Team Viper, take out the barracks. These guys are mercenaries, mostly criminals, and they'll fight like the sociopaths they are. Stay above in the darkness; use the Gatling on anything that moves until Team Cobra gives the all clear to land. You secure the gate. No one leaves."

He paused and looked at his wife.

"OK. Set your watches. Mark! We arrive in Basseterre at 0415."

The teams separated. Quietly they loaded ammunition and equipment on each of their respective jet-powered stealth helicopters. They came and went, each one reaching up and touching the banner on the firewall of their machine.

TRUE BELIEVERS

"No Cubans on this one," Quinn said softly to Debra and Richard. "Even Fidel thinks his Special Forces are infiltrated."

• • •

Wire-Rim pushed the evening treatment into Doctor Blue's IV port and sneered. "Sweet dreams." A.W. listened to the metallic click of the lock securing the metal door. Then his mind drifted to never-never land, watching Rita running naked in a field of monarch butterflies. The butterflies followed her wherever she ran.

"Doctor Blue!"

A.W. opened his eyes. A young lady with long, blond hair stood beside his bed, yellow courtyard light shining on her back through the lone, barred window. She looked down at him with glowing, soft, blue eyes.

"Who are you?"

"My name is Janet Sue."

A.W. turned his head toward the locked door.

"How'd you get in here…you're a hallucination!"

Then she touched him on the forehead with her fingers and A.W.'s mind instantly cleared from the chemical fog. He sat up.

"Your friends are coming to rescue you tonight, doctor. I want you to go downstairs and find Norah. Stay with her. Tonight will be very frightening for her."

"They'll see me from the surveillance room."

She smiled.

"Both guards in the video room are napping."

Janet Sue walked to the door and opened it, waving for A.W. to follow.

"When your hope has turned to dust," she said, walking beside A.W., "that is when those who truly love you come to your rescue."

She smiled again before she left him, walking up the stairs to the third floor.

Walking down the stairs, Doctor A.W. Blue felt invincible.

CHAPTER 13

WORDS HE USES

Jim Morrison looked up from his office desk at Amy Hamilton just standing there in his pharmacy. He glanced at the day planner and up at her.

"I'm busy," he said. "Sorry."

"This won't take long Jim. Just wanted to stop by and thank you for your support. I think you will be pleased with the money your department will save, switching companies."

"It's Mr. Tiffany's decision. He made the decision."

"Well. I'm sure he valued your opinion and Stanley's."

…Tiffany…who got to Tiffany…what the hell…call Vladimir…

Jim blew into his coffee cup and sipped, looking at Amy.

"Stanley wanted to stay with Horizon."

She turned toward the office door and walked with a deliberate loud clicking of her heels down the hall.

"So did I," Jim shouted.

The pharmacy staff watched, with amusement, the slender drug representative wearing a form-fitting blue dress, strutting past, her speed slowed by the dress, limiting the length of her stride.

"She oughta hike that dress up a bit," a pharmacy tech chuckled to the chief pharmacist.

…OK…so you want to make this personal…so you want to play games…Stanley. You're outta your league…

She slammed shut the green car door.

…poor dufus is going to regret this…

●●●

Danielle got home before Chloe and Stanley. She got the mail and sorted through it.

…electricity bill…cable bill…ad for crap…ad for crap…clear skin for Chloe…wonder why she ordered that, she doesn't have acne…

Danielle tossed the small white box addressed to Chloe Norma McMillen on her daughter's bed.

"There's a package for some sort of acne medicine you ordered on your bed," Danielle said during dinner.

"Came in the mail."

Chloe looked slightly confused.

"OK."

After dinner, Stanley helped Danielle clean the kitchen.

"I'm going to light a heater and have a Cuban and Basil's outside," he said, starting the dishwasher.

"I'm going to my room and finish a book report," Chloe said.

"It's kinda chilly," Danielle said.

"It'll be fine, no wind. Come on out." He winked at his wife.

"Maybe."

Danielle stared at her husband standing under the gas heater on the deck, looking down at the city lights in the valley, smoking a cigar given to him by President Castro, and sipping on his favorite whiskey.

…I love you…let's get far away from here…

"MOM! MOM, come here!"

"What?" Danielle asked, looking through Chloe's open bedroom door.

"Mom…" Chloe held a cell phone toward her mother.

Danielle sat on her daughter's bed. She scrolled through the text messages that Chloe had just read. Then she put the phone on the bed.

"It's dad and that drug lady texting love stuff to each other."

Danielle chewed on her thumbnail.

"Your daddy didn't write this garbage, honey."

"How do you know?"

"Wait here."

Danielle went to her dressing room and took a shirt box covered with Christmas paper from the shelf above her dresses.

Chloe watched Danielle remove the cover. Her mother's fingers trembled.

"I've saved these letters your daddy wrote me from the very beginning," Danielle whispered, handing several open letters to her daughter.

"This is how your daddy woos a lady…these are the words he uses, the way he puts sentences together…not that soap opera crap on this cell phone."

Chloe read three letters before looking at her mother.

"Yup, Mom. What're you gonna do?"

"What we are going to do, honey, is march right out there in the cold and hug your daddy real hard and have a drink with him and love him."

"Can I have what you're having?"

"You sure can."

"Then what?"

"I'm going to call a dear friend of ours, and give him this phone. That's what I'm going to do, Chloe. I'm going to fix this."

●●●

Stanley had retrieved a second Basil Hayden's. Danielle opened the French doors, and Stanley watched his wife and daughter walking toward him, each with a glass of red wine in their hands.

CHAPTER 14

A Celebration In Heaven

Three sleek, black helicopters, invisible to radar, lifted from Key West International Airport at 0130 hours on a moonless night, their jet engines roaring softly. Flying in formation, they flew south over Cuba, headed for St. Kitts at 400 miles per hour.

The compound glowed with sodium lights, giving a yellow hue to the sky. The attack, precise as a surgeon's scalpel, took place at 0415 hours, exactly as planned.

The machine gun turrets exploded and crumpled to the ground the same instant a laser-guided bomb breached the barracks' roof, followed by the roar of a Gatling gun.

In the midst of the turmoil, the helicopter with team Mongoose landed only ten yards from the three-story building.

The side door dropped. Richard charged out first and past two dead guards lying next to the front door. Quinn and Debra followed and then nine True Believers.

Richard opened the front door with his left hand, his pistol raised.

Standing in the long hallway with their arms raised above their heads, stood forty young ladies in various stages of undress. In front of the girls stood a frail, whiskered, old man, his right arm around a teenager.

Richard pushed his pistol into a pocket and walked to Norah. When she recognized him, Norah Chase ran and leapt into his arms, quivering.

"A.W.?" Quinn questioned.

Debra looked at her husband.

"A.W.! Is that you?" He walked toward the old man.

"Yes, Quinn; been a long time."

Richard and Deb, who had heard the legendary tales of Doctor Blue, watched the two old friends embrace.

"What the hell, A.W.?"

"Long story. Hell does exist, Quinn."

Wire-Rim descended the stairs and pushed through the congested hallway, his right arm extended, holding a pistol tightly against the head of a lady with long, blond hair. His left hand held her tightly, wrapped around and around with blond hair.

"Let me leave, or I blow her brains out," Wire-Rim said. "I'm not kidding."

It happened when he took the pistol he held in his right hand away from Janet Sue's head and pointed it at Norah Chase.

With the intent of evil spewing from his eyes, Wire-Rim placed Norah, wrapped in Richard's arms, in his gun sight. He pulled the trigger.

His numb trigger finger refused to twitch. The gun did not fire. He moved his confused eyes down toward his hand. Then his entire right arm prickled with dysfunction.

At that instant, Debra fired her pistol. It did not occur to this former DEA agent that she might miss, that she might hit one of the ladies standing around the evil man. Instinctively, she saw a man she loved with a trembling young lady in his arms, defenseless, and she pulled the trigger.

The young ladies all around did not scream when the wire-rimmed glasses flew backward and they were showered by bits of skull and brain, splattering on their faces.

Debra did not think. She simply pointed her .45 cal loaded with hollow point bullets and blew the evil man's head into tiny pieces. She watched the man crumple toward the floor, his left hand entangled in the long, blond hair, pulling the woman over. She watched Janet Sue untangle her hair from the dead man's fingers. Then Debra looked at Quinn.

Quinn formed the word "WOW" with his lips. No sound came out.

Richard, still hugging Norah, said, "Thank-you." It took three attempts before a sound came through his lips.

The girls began to cheer, seeing their tormentor, the man who injected them daily with opiates, the man who sometimes raped them, lying on the floor in an enlarging pool of blood coming from his destroyed skull.

A.W. cleared his throat.

"Quinn, it's a long story, but we are all addicted to narcotics. We can't leave here and go cold turkey."

"OK, A.W. Got a medical evac plane coming. We'll get you all to Bethesda."

Doctor Blue smiled. "You've always impressed the hell out of me, Quinn," He turned to his right to look at Debra and Richard.

"A.W., meet my wife Debra and my good friend, Richard."

"It is my honor to meet you," he said, shaking Debra's hand. "Thanks for saving my life."

He walked to Richard, his arms still around Norah tightly. He leaned down and kissed her on the forehead. "Told you we would be rescued."

"No...you didn't!"

"Well, I thought it."

A.W. straightened up and studied Richard's scarred face and one good eye.

"You are the mighty Richard Elmore Fortin that Norah told me would come and rescue her. When I asked how, she always said, 'You'll see.' I am honored to meet a fellow Yankees fan."

Richard smiled his crooked smile. He removed the dirty Yankees hat and placed it on Norah's head.

"I'm not. It's for Norah. I brought it for Norah. It's a souvenir of the day she was rescued, and a reminder to never give up...ever."

Norah put her head tight against Richard's chest and squeezed.

Janet Sue watched and then came close to Quinn.

"There's a computer on the third level. He set it on fire." She nodded at the body sprawled on the concrete floor.

"Thanks. Who are you, exactly?"

Debra leaned close to her husband. "Her name is Janet Sue."

"And I thought you were just a legend."

"I am, Captain Quinn O'Malley. I am," Janet Sue smiled, while combing bloody particles from her hair with her fingers. She walked to the stairwell and up the stairs.

"We thought you were dead, A.W. We searched and then the Cuban Navy looked for a week. Finally, your boat washed up on shore. We all thought you were dead."

"I have been, Quinn, quite dead."

"Team Viper to Robin Hood," the radio cracked.

"Go ahead, Team Viper."

"The chief of police has arrived; wants to know what's going on."

"Tell the chief that Quinn says he should take a vacation, that he never saw a thing, because he had left on vacation."

"He's leaving."

● ● ●

The ringing cell phone next to her face beside the pillow awakened Belvia Chase. She wiped a little pool of saliva from the screen on the pillowcase and looked. She did not recognize the number.

"HI, MOM!" Norah Chase shouted into Richard's yellow transceiver.

"Norah is safe. We'll be home tomorrow. She is not hurt."

Belvia could not answer.

· · ·

"I think we've made some powerful individuals very unhappy," Quinn muttered to Richard and Debra, walking to their helicopter. He carried a scorched PC in his arms, the melted power cord dangling. "I wonder how she put the fire out?"

Debra smiled. "There's a celebration in heaven today, guys. We've done good."

Norah walked between Richard and Doctor Blue, holding their hands.

They climbed into the helicopter and Norah put both hands on the banner.

"True Believers," she said. "You told me a secret when I was eight, about the True Believers," Norah said, looking at Richard. "I always thought you made it up." She hugged him with both arms.

Quinn fastened his seat belt and leaned towards Richard. "They will come looking for us, you know."

"I'd like that," Richard replied.

CHAPTER 15

BREAKING NEWS

The Wednesday evening poker players had assembled on either side of the long table, parallel to the bar. The TV above the bar flashed moving pictures with the sound off. Carla Fife played the old upright piano, missing one black key, taking requests. The red and yellow theater popcorn machine in the corner next to the front door made pop…pop…popping sounds, being loaded and emptied by Chloe and Timothy's son, Charles. He took a large, paper bucket, filled with extra butter and salt, to his mother playing the piano.

"The Usual Suspects" along with Stanley, Doctor Smith, Chief of Police Strait, Doctor Varner and Doctor McCaferty, sat at the long poker table, watching Timothy fill glass mugs with draft beer, a green towel over his right shoulder. Machete presided at the far end, with Little Miss at his side, shuffling cards.

Danielle, Ramona, and two ER nurses, Jillena and Patti, talked in the corner booth.

"I think Chloe and Charles are enamored with each other," Ramona commented, watching the young man walk back to the popcorn machine after delivering a hot supply to their booth.

Danielle watched, too.

"I'll be happy when Katie is back," Jillena said, watching the Cronkite kids line up for more popcorn after getting permission from Doug.

"I hope after they find Norah, Belvia just moves right back here," Patti said, and everyone in the booth agreed.

"Look at those kids," Danielle said in the direction of the pop-corn line. "You'd never guess they are adopted."

Machete won the first two hands. The rest of the table protested and demanded that Little Miss be put back in her room, to no avail.

"How's your pacemaker pocket?" Doctor McCaferty reached across the table and pulled Doug's shirt open over the left chest.

"Nothing a little Tylenol can't handle."

Doctor McCaferty grinned. "That looks pretty, Doug," then added, "you should notice improvement in your breathing soon. We'll fine-tune it and do an ECHO when you come in next month."

"I feel stronger already. Been sleeping all night without sitting in the chair!"

"Good."

"Turn the sound on!" Pete yelled, looking up at the television showing a *BREAKING NEWS* announcement.

Carla stopped playing.

Timothy pointed the remote toward the Magnavox and turned the sound up.

"We interrupt this program to bring you a breaking development. We go live to Ronald Reagan Washington National Airport and Jill Rodimaker."

The young lady held a microphone, staring into the bright camera lights, standing next to a United States Air Force Medivac turboprop.

"Sometime in the past twenty-four hours, forty young women were rescued from a human trafficking cartel on the island of St. Kitts. Details remain murky at this point about how long this sex trade has been in operation or even who rescued these ladies, many of whom are teenagers…Here they come now!"

The television camera panned away from the reporter and onto the young ladies walking single file from the plane toward a line of green, unmarked vans idling with their doors open.

Behind the ladies, walked three men: an elderly frail man with two other men – one taller with curly hair and a Hemingway beard, holding a lady's hand, and a shorter man whose face showed a large scar up his right cheek, ending at the hair line, holding the hand of a teenager wearing a dirty New York Yankee's baseball hat.

"Jill Rodimaker from WTXT News 44." The reporter thrust her microphone into Norah Chase's face. "Please tell the American public what happened…Were you being held prisoner, young lady?"

Without warning or hesitation, Richard Elmore Fortin reached and took the microphone from the reporter. He turned and spoke directly toward the camera.

"This is not a pretty face," he said, pointing with the index finger of his free hand at the scar and glass eye. "It is not a face one easily forgets," he continued. "To the evil ones, the ones with corrupt black souls, you that sell sex and narcotics for pleasure and profit, I say memorize this face. It will be the last face you see, right before you see the face of God."

He handed the microphone back to the reporter.

"That should piss them off," he muttered to Quinn.

"Yup. That'll help. Don't think the scumbags believe in God, Richard."

"They will," Richard replied. "I've met him."

"You just stirred up a nest of vipers," Doctor Blue said, "venomous vipers."

Richard gently grasped the old man, turning him face to face.

He winked at Doctor A.W. Blue with his good eye.

●●●

They sat in silence at Poor Joe's for several minutes. Timothy muted the TV and they listened to the popcorn machine without speaking.

"That old man is Doctor Blue," Stanley finally broke the silence.

"Holy shit," exclaimed Doug. "That was O'Malley and Fortin with him!"

"That blond girl holding Richard's hand is Norah Chase," Danielle said. "They've found her!"

• • •

Stanley's pocket vibrated. The guys around the table watched him answer the yellow Comstat phone.

"Hi Stanley, Quinn here. You see the evening news?"

"Just did. We're all here at Poor Joe's."

"Poker night."

"Yup."

"Need for you to get a couple of beds ready. The sons of bitches have A.W. and Norah addicted. Have to ease them through the withdrawal."

"I'm on it," Stanley replied. He turned and motioned to Ramona.

"We need two ICU beds, Ramona."

The director of nurses called the hospital.

CHAPTER 16

COMFORTING PLACE

There are people in Big Bay who believe the old building is somehow alive and has a soul. The Usual Suspects quietly believe. So too, do complete strangers, after several adult beverages, admitting the building has "a feel."

Poor Joe's is located on Union Street, with Basswood Street on one side and Grant on the other. The Big Bay river runs behind it and is connected by a brick tunnel which exits on the steep clay river bank just below the dam.

Built in 1898 by Irish immigrants, the building served as a whiskey depot. Joe McCain purchased the building in 1929. During prohibition he advertised it as a "dance hall." The apartments upstairs were laughingly labeled "the consolation rooms." When pressed on the questionable activities taking place in a Catholic community, Joe simply answered, "All God's children need love."

During the forbidden years, Irish whiskey and Cuban rum were transported through the tunnel from the river under the cover of darkness. When Prohibition ended in 1933, Joe painted POOR JOE'S BAR with green paint on a white metal sign and hung it over the front door. It has not been touched since, and the lettering is barely visible on the rusty sign, especially at night, even though it has a spotlight shining on it.

The wooden floor is scarred. It sports dark stains from blood oozing into the cracks, the result of Doug shooting several members of the HELL'S SPAWN motorcycle gang from New York City when they disrupted a private retirement party for Norma Bouvier. The buckshot holes remain, too. The long poker table sits over that stain and the holes. And there is a dark stain in the hallway, outside the men's room, where Machete Juarez had lain after being shot in the head by a teenager. The newest stain is near the front door, where Jesus Veracruz died after being shot while planting a bomb in the middle of the night. Blind Machete, using a double-barreled shotgun, had accurately aimed the gun as directed by Little Miss.

The old bar knows the agony of death and the joy of life. Great celebrations and weddings have taken place there. So too, have prayer meetings and heavy discussions concerning life and death. The True Believers have met at Poor Joe's on occasion before undertaking their "reckonings."

It is a comforting place. Despite the situation, people feel safe inside. Even Fidel Castro felt safe. And he found his wife there, taking the bar's beloved cook, Dora, back to Havana with him.

Now they once again gathered, sitting around the long poker table and the booths, and the two round tables, now pulled close to the long table; their minds processing what their eyes had just witnessed. Doctor A.W. Blue had been thought drowned off the shore of Cuba ten years ago, his aluminum boat found washed up on the north shore of Cuba. Sweet Norah Chase, now a beautiful young teenager (She had lived in the house next to the Methodist Church with her mom, brother, and sister for a while after Katie had insisted on going to Alaska and bringing them back on Quinn O'Malley's plane) had been kidnapped and now rescued by Quinn and Richard from a human trafficking cartel.

Sitting in silence, everyone knew exactly who the unknown rescuers were. The True Believers had intervened in their lives before.

Stanley and Danielle now sat close to each other. "I'm sure grateful we met Quinn O'Malley that night at the Green Parrot," Danielle said.

She leaned forward, touching her forehead against her husband's.

Chloe McMillen and Charles Fife sat in the corner booth next to the popcorn machine, shoes off, watching, their toes touching under the table.

CHAPTER 17

MONSTER

Debra knocked on Belvia's front door.

Katie moved the shade aside and peeked through the front window. "Deb's here."

"Norah?"

"She's alone."

Katie opened the front door and the three friends merged on the front porch.

"Where's Norah?" Belvia asked.

"On a plane with Quinn and Richard headed to Big Bay."

"WHY!?"

Debra and Katie led Belvia to the couch and sat her down, and each sat on either side of Belvia.

"She needs to be hospitalized for a little while. Her kidnappers gave her drugs. She's addicted. Quinn wants her at Big Bay General with friends while she goes through withdrawal."

"Oh sweet Jesus." Belvia's voice trembled. "What have they done to my little girl?"

"She's OK. She's not hurt. Belvia, they were saving her for some prince who only buys virgins."

Belvia shuddered, and Katie's blue eyes flashed with anger.

"I hugged her. She has a feisty sparkle in those blue eyes of hers. She's clinging to Richard like he's Jesus Christ."

Belvia looked down without speaking, watching her own tears

splash on the floor before finally saying, "Well, Deb, I bet he was sent by Jesus. I love that man."

"I do, too," Debra replied.

…huddled…helpless…Norah's eyes pleading…Richard's eye swearing…the pistol pointed…hateful red eyes…that bastard's head exploding…a watermelon at target practice…

"Kids at school?"

"Yes."

"Let's go get 'em. Mike is waiting outside in the Suburban. He'll fly us to Big Bay."

"The kids love flying on that plane," Belvia said, drying her eyes with a Kleenex and blowing her nose.

● ● ●

Stanley and Jack McCaferty stood on the tarmac, watching the needle-nosed jet circle Big Bay Airport twice and then begin its landing approach.

"I'm worried about A.W.," Stanley said.

"He's been through what would kill most of us," Jack replied.

The plane landed and whooshed past them toward the end of the runway.

"Quinn's assigned a guard to his room and at the entrances to the hospital."

"I noticed: guys in black Suburbans."

"Quinn said to me, 'Stanley, I'm putting a guard on Norah, too. I just received some initial information retrieved from a computer we secured from St. Kitts. We're dealing with a monster.'"

Stanley paused, watching the plane turn and head in their direction.

"He's worried, Jack, because A.W. and Norah can identify people who will kill in order to prevent exposure."

Jack looked at Stanley.

"Oh…shit."

"He had them both flown here because everybody knows each other and any strangers in town will be obvious."

"He's one smart man, Stanley."

●●●

Belvia ran down the hospital hallway toward her daughter's room. A man wearing a Caribbean Soul T-shirt stood from the chair next to room 439, his right hand touching the handle of his side-arm, blocking the way into Norah's room.

"It's her mother, Emanuel. It's OK," Quinn shouted, following down the hall with Stanley, Debra and Katie.

Not a word between mother and daughter; their two bodies merged into one on the hospital bed. Belvia accidently snagged the IV line in her daughter's left arm, pulling it out. They lay together, blood dripping onto the white sheets. They breathed in unison.

...this is how I felt the day I gave birth to you...

"Hi mom."

Belvia kissed her daughter's cheek.

Richard watched from the chair next to Norah's bed, his jaw tightening and relaxing, over and over.

...I absolutely adore that woman...

Quinn O'Malley grasped his wife's hand in his then reached and took Katie's hand, and the three of them stood looking, just inside the room, holding hands and watching.

Wyatt Tiffany poked his head through the open door. He looked at Norah and Belvia lying on the bed.

"I hear you've been through quite an ordeal, young lady. So happy to see you here, safe and sound."

The hairs on the back of Stanley's neck stood up. He turned his head and looked at Quinn.

"Who's that?" Quinn asked when the administrator walked away.

"Wyatt Tiffany, our new administrator."

Stanley watched Quinn's weathered face, his eyes widening.

CHAPTER 18

GRANDPA

Amy Hamilton nodded off in the darkness, driving east on Murfreesboro Road in Franklin, Tennessee, toward I-65, heading back to Big Bay. Her chin tickled against her blouse, and she startled awake. Three hours at the IHOP, meeting two men; both were hesitant, initially, before being charmed and signing a lease and contract for pain clinic number twelve. Amy hated pancakes. She ate a tall stack during the negotiations, smiling and conversing with a hint of southern drawl.

…should NOT have eaten…more coffee…damn I'm tired…damn this headache…

She reached for her porcelain travel mug in the center console while glancing in the rearview and slamming the brakes, causing her green Volvo to slide sideways into the shoulder gravel before coming to a stop.

Amy stared in the rearview mirror at the fixed glass eye and then at the scar.

…damn…damn…damn…

"Get out!" she screamed. "Get the hell out of my car! You need money? Here!" She grabbed frantically into her purse then threw two crumpled hundred dollar bills into the back seat. "Now GET OUT!"

Richard rubbed the skin under his glass eye and wiped away the tears that chronically drained.

Amy reached into her purse again.

"Bring your hand out, empty," Richard said. "Slowly."

She twisted, looking at Richard from between the bucket seats.

"Who are you?" Her eyes focused on a revolver in his right hand, resting in his lap.

…think…think, Amy…

Richard shrugged.

With the twist of her left wrist, Amy turned on the interior lights. Her body rotated in the driver's seat, looking at Richard's face. She gasped a little before uttering, "You were on television… with those rescued girls."

"Remember what I said?"

A Tennessee State Trooper pulled his car behind the green Volvo. He turned on the cruiser's overhead flashing lights.

…NOW…!

Amy opened the door and flung herself out, onto the pavement, screaming, "He's got a gun! He's got a gun! Rapist! He's got a gun!" She waved toward Richard.

The officer approached the Volvo, his sidearm drawn, aiming directly at Richard's head.

"Let me see your hands; both hands on your head. Do it now!"

Richard slid to the driver's side. The officer opened the door, the gun still pointing at Richard's head.

"Get out and lie face down on the pavement, arms out."

The trooper yanked first the left arm and then the right to the small of Richard's back and cuffed his wrists. He poked his head through the open back door and saw the revolver on the rear seat. He grabbed it.

…well, Richard…this is going well…

Richard rested his cheek on the Tennessee gravel.

A second state police car arrived with two troopers. The three troopers discussed something out of earshot.

"OK, Miss Hamilton, you need to follow me back to the state police post in Franklin. I'll take your statement and finish the report."

"And you," the trooper said to Richard, lifting him off the pavement by his shackled arms, "get to go to jail." He pushed Richard toward the two newly arrived troopers.

"Remember what I said!" Richard shouted at Amy.

"You shut up," the fat trooper said, pushing Richard's head down into the back seat.

●●●

"What's this?" the evidence department deputy asked in the processing room, patting Richard's pockets and removing his Comstat phone. He turned the yellow triangular phone around and over with a puzzled look.

"My cell phone."

"Never seen a phone like this."

"It's new."

"Looks expensive."

"It is. I'm allowed one call, right?"

The deputy pointed toward a pay phone on the painted concrete wall.

"I'm broke, please let me make my call on this," Richard pleaded.

"How can you afford a phone like this and be broke? You steal this?"

"A birthday gift. Sentimental attachments. You can place the call for me. I just need to let Grandpa know where I am."

"Thought you'd want to call for a lawyer."

"I'm not from around here. Born and raised in Michigan. Just let me tell Grandpa."

He handed Richard the phone, watching him closely but mostly staring at the scar on his face and the eyelid that did not blink.

Richard punched a sequence of buttons, ending with Q.

Quinn rolled over, untangling himself from Debra's arm, and looked at the message screen.

"What, Richard?"

"Hi, Grandpa. Johnny here. I'm in the Franklin, Tennessee jail."

"Why?"

"Charge of attempted rape."

"I'll take care of it."

"Thanks, Grandpa."

Richard handed the yellow phone back to the processing deputy. "Thank you. I'll need this when I leave."

"Mister Saint James, I reckon where you're headed, you ain't gonna ever need any of these things for a very long time," he said, looking at Richard's driver's license.

Richard smiled.

...yup, Richard, this night is going well...

●●●

Amy Hamilton took several deep breaths before turning the ignition key.

...that should take care of that creep for a while...one scary bastard...I'm going to Chicago first...what the hell, Vladimir...that glass eye freaked me out...damn this headache...

She noticed her hands trembling.

...wish I still smoked...

●●●

During Richard's arraignment, the judge denied bail. His court-appointed attorney protested.

"Look at him," the judge retorted. "You want the likes of him on your porch, taking your beautiful daughter, Elisabeth, out on a date? And, Mister Willie, your client is a significant flight risk; admits he ain't from these parts. No bail; bail denied."

Richard stared at the pudgy judge. When the judge slammed his gavel and stared back, Richard winked with his good eye.

"CONTEMPT!" the judge yelled, slamming the gavel a second

time. "That was contempt right there, deputies. Please show Mister Saint James what we think of northern contempt here in the great state of Tennessee.

…what a sorry excuse for a judge…you haven't seen contempt… yet…

● ● ●

Three stealth XS-1 helicopters flew over the Williamson County Jail in Franklin, Tennessee, at midnight. Two helicopters landed in a vacant field across the street from the Rolling Hills Community Church. The third hovered high above the jail, jamming all radio frequencies, electronics, and phone communications.

Twenty men, dressed completely in black, trotted down Beasley Drive to Century Court. When they reached the county jail front door, Quinn held a strange looking metal device next to the lock. It made several clicking sounds. The door opened and the men entered.

The deputy behind the bullet-proof glass looked up. He started to reach toward a large red button on the desk next to the phone then froze and raised his hands over his head, facing a rocket propelled grenade launcher. The dispatcher sitting next to him reached for the transmit button on the radio console.

"DON'T," the first deputy said to the dispatcher. "Look!"

They both stood with their arms raised.

"Open the door," Quinn demanded.

The dispatcher pushed the proper button.

"Come on in."

"Where's the inmate who was arraigned today before Judge Fonda for attempted rape?" Quinn asked calmly, fingering his pistol.

"You guys know how much trouble you're in?" the night deputy replied.

"Where is he?"

"Solitary. Cell one."

Two deputies charged into the hallway from the video surveillance room, guns in their hands. Both their pistols bounced on the tile floor, coming face to face with twenty men in black carrying automatic weapons.

Quinn unlocked the solitary confinement cell and pulled open the heavy door with a tiny window.

"Grandpa's here, son; let's go." And he gave Richard a wink, pushing the four deputies into the cell and locking it.

"Looks like they did a little fine-tuning on your face," Quinn said, while trotting back to the idling helicopters.

"Southern hospitality, Quinn, on the house. Think it helped?"

"Maybe."

"I memorized their faces, too. Where we headed?"

"Big Bay. We've got a problem."

"Let's go." Richard grinned a swollen, stiff smile. "The folks from Tennessee will be looking for John Allen Saint James from Marquette, Michigan."

"That's a new one." Quinn chuckled, handing Richard the yellow Comstat phone and his wallet.

"How'd you find it?"

"Evidence room, all logged and tagged." Quinn grinned. "We erased the hard drives on all three surveillance cameras. Like you say, hard to forget a face like yours."

Richard shook his head.

"Here's a Tennessee souvenir." Quinn handed Richard a folded white paper.

Richard shook his head again, looking at his fingerprints.

The helicopters lifted, heading north, and joined the third, flying in formation at 400 miles per hour and invisible to radar.

Quinn leaned close to Richard so he could hear. "We finished decoding and downloading the information from the St. Kitts computer yesterday."

He coughed and cleared his throat.

"This onion's got many layers, Richard."

"I still need to have that conversation with Amy Hamilton."

"Yes, you do."

Quinn paused.

"I put double guards on A.W. and Norah – one outside the room, one inside."

Richard looked at Quinn.

"The new administrator, Tiffany, complained to Chief Strait; said it made the other patients and his staff uncomfortable. Wanted them removed."

"What'd Chief Strait say?"

"He drove to the hospital and deputized our guys. Guess that Tiffany fellow blew a gasket."

He paused again.

"We've got a major problem, Richard."

CHAPTER 19

MUTATED VIRUSES

"Turn the TV volume loud," Quinn said in Timothy's direction, "just in case our sweep missed a bug."

The CLOSED FOR INVENTORY sign hung from Poor Joe's locked front door, flapping a little in the morning breeze.

Drs. McCaferty and Smith had their receptionists reschedule the day's appointments, citing an emergency situation.

Victor Bonifacio flew in from St. Paul. Rose joined them, traveling from Las Vegas.

They sat at the long poker table: the Usual Suspects, along with Quinn, Debra, and Chief Strait.

"What happened?" Doug pointed at the bruises on Richard's face.

"Cosmetic adjustments, Doug."

"I'm sure it'll be fine after the swelling goes down," Wayne added.

Quinn spoke softly in a somber tone, unlike anything his old friend Vincent could remember.

"There are days…"

He took a deep breath.

"…when I think I've seen everything." Quinn blew on his cup then sipped the black Cuban coffee with two sugar lumps.

"Then we download the hard drive from St. Kitts, and I shake my head and say, 'Quinn, you ain't seen nothing yet.'"

The television blared the sound of Andy and Barney arguing about the best time of day to go fishing.

"It's hard to fathom where all the arms of this enormous beast reach. It's simply referred to as *The Company*. We've been able to decode a few names and their offshore accounts in the Cayman Islands, but it's arduous business, cracking this encryption."

He took another sip.

On the television, Barney bet Andy he could catch more fish in the evening than Andy could in the morning.

"What we have been able to glean so far is that we are facing a multifaceted business dealing in legal drugs – furnished to hospitals, doctors offices, and pain clinics – illegal street drug distribution, as well as the sex trade – human trafficking and prostitution."

He stared at his friends around the table.

"And that's not the worst of it." His complexion grew paler. "It gets worse."

"Coven Pharmaceuticals has a covert research and development department. Their scientists are working on a nightmare at a biological research complex in Matagalpa, Nicaragua."

Quinn's eyes glistened.

On the television, Andy held up a stringer of trout: six brook and one rainbow. Barney held a stringer with one sunfish.

Quinn reached into his shirt pocket and tossed two thumb drives on the table.

"They have hybridized tiger mosquitoes and infected them with a mutated H1N3 influenza virus; call it the CAI virus, standing for coronary artery inflammation. They intentionally infected a remote village in northern South Africa. Eighty percent of the village experienced joint pain, cephalalgia, and chest pain. Nearly fifty percent of those infected died within a week from myocardial infarction, regardless of the subject's age – kids, young people; it didn't matter."

Doctor McCaferty uttered an epitaph softly.

"Why?" Chief Strait asked. "What's the point?"

"There's evidence they're working on a vaccine. Not sure if they're planning to start an epidemic and then come to the rescue with a miraculous vaccine, making billions, or if this is a biological weapon, or maybe both," Quinn replied, moving the thumb drives in a circle around and around his coffee mug with his forefinger.

Doctor Smith shook his head and rubbed his neck. "This is unconscionable."

"The infected ones who survived were left with pulmonary hypertension and renal insufficiency. I checked with an old buddy at the Center for Disease Control. She confirmed a mysterious outbreak of what's been labeled malaria by a local doctor in Tshipise, South Africa, last April. I double-checked with a friend at the World Health Organization. He confirmed 'some sort of outbreak that appeared to be self-limited;' his only concern is that it seemed particularly lethal."

"How much of this virus do they have, can you tell?" Debra asked, looking at her husband.

"Nope, no idea…or the locations."

"They may be planning to use this as a blackmail tool," Debra continued, "holding hostage any government not willing to play ball with them. I saw that kind of blackmailing plenty when I worked with the DEA, only they used bombs and assassins. Good God, Quinn."

"Yup. Good thought."

Machete sat at the end of the poker table, his forehead resting on the hardwood, listening. Little Miss licked his hand. He lifted his head, which now had a red pressure area in the middle of his forehead.

"I have known this darkness, in my youth. I took assignments from evil men coveting power. That is the reason I first came to Big Bay; I came to destroy and you saved me. This I can tell you, my amigos, the creature is a giant octopus with tentacles reaching into places you never would dream possible."

He stroked Little Miss who now watched his face.

"The many arms of the beast cannot be defeated. It is the head, amigos; wherever it is, you must remove the head. The arms will twitch without direction, if the head is gone."

"We have deciphered a few names so far," Quinn said. "Stanley, does the name Andrew Hamilton ring a bell?"

Stanley shivered.

"Yes, Quinn. He owned the Montgomery Ward's store in Big Bay and a hardware store where Radio Shack is now before he sold and moved to New York. I dated his daughter, Amy."

Wendell looked up from his coffee cup and felt sorry for his friend.

...poor guy...

"James Hamilton is the majority stockholder for Coven Pharmaceuticals."

Machete felt Stanley's trembling.

Quinn hesitated and then stood. He walked to the end of the table and put his hand on Stanley's shoulder.

Stanley tilted his head up and looked at Quinn's eyes.

"Your wife's father, Wayne Prudhomme, was a hospital administrator in New Orleans."

"Yes."

"Danielle's father was a stockholder in Coven; Danielle is a stockholder, Stan."

"Her inheritance...It's her inheritance...Well, at least part of it...shit!"

Stanley twisted his head around and looked at up at his old friend.

Quinn nodded.

"Wyatt Tiffany is a major stockholder, too," Quinn continued. "And to complete our little Big Bay circle, your old girlfriend, Amy, is a stockholder."

...my wife and my high school sweetheart...Jesus help me...

"Curiouser and curiouser," Doctor McCaferty exclaimed. "Alice has just fallen through the looking glass." He stood and walked behind the bar for a larger glass of Jameson Irish Whiskey. He stretched to the high shelf, reaching for the rare bottle filled with liquor aged eighteen years.

Timothy watched Jack pour a tall glass and smiled.

Victor Bonifacio watched Quinn twiddle with the thumb drives. "By now, they must know we have their computer and thumb drives."

"Very true," Quinn replied, aiming the red-colored one at Victor and sending it down the table with the flick of his forefinger.

"We managed to decipher that one, Victor," he said, pointing at the red thumb drive in Victor's hand. "This one," he held the black one, "has some sort of German encryption that we haven't figured out."

Quinn turned his head toward Doctor Smith. "When will A.W. be up for a little conversation?"

"I'm weaning the phenobarbital drip off this afternoon. Tomorrow, Quinn."

"Tomorrow." Quinn looked at Drs. McCaferty, Smith and then toward Stanley. "Tomorrow we have a conversation."

CHAPTER 20

ROTTEN CAULDRON

"What's wrong, Daddy?"

Chloe looked through the open den door; then she walked in.

Stanley sat behind his century-old oak desk. His shoulders slumped. He held a water glass filled with ice cubes and whiskey. A partly emptied bottle of Basil Hayden's sat next to the telephone.

…I hate her…

Stanley looked up with his eyes without raising his head. Chloe walked around the desk and wrapped both arms around her father.

"I'm sorry for whatever it is, daddy. Is it that lady who's trying to blackmail us?"

"Kinda related, honey."

"Mom's taking care of it."

"What?"

"Mom says she's calling a friend. Mom's going to fix it."

Stanley hugged his daughter, looked at her face, and hugged her again.

…she's so damn much like her mom…

"Love you, Chloe."

"Love you. Everything's gonna be OK."

Chloe glanced back, leaving the den, and then stopped

"Can I have a taste?"

"That would be against the law."

"Yeah, right."

Chloe closed the den door and sat in the chair next to her father's desk. She brought her knees up, resting her chin on them. Then she shook her head just a little, allowing her shoulder length auburn hair to hang down on either knee and looked at him with kind hazel eyes.

...so much like Danielle...the older she gets...so much...

Stanley pulled open the bottom left drawer. The old oak stuck a little as he pulled. Finally, he opened it enough and reached in, retrieving a Jack Daniel's sipping glass.

Chloe watched her father extend two fingers into his tall glass and fish out three ice cubes, carefully placing them in the Jack Daniel's glass. She watched Stanley ceremoniously pour just a little of the golden Basil Hayden's over the ice cubes before handing her the little glass.

They raised their glasses, clinking gently.

"Here's to everything being OK."

Stanley watched his nearly sixteen-year-old daughter fill her mouth with his favorite bourbon and hold it for several seconds before swallowing.

"Whew!" Chloe exclaimed. "That's warm! And delicious."

"I'll buy you a bottle when you're twenty-one."

Chloe smiled.

"Our own private communion. When life sucks, this is what we need to do, have our communion."

Stanley smiled. "OK."

"You gonna tell mom?"

"Yup, she'll get a kick out of it."

"OK, dad."

"Wait, honey, I have something for you."

Chloe watched her father carefully peel the copper band with the large silver bH initials from the Basil Hayden's bottle. He connected the opposing ends and reached for his daughter's left arm.

Chloe had never seen that tender expression on her father's

face. He carefully slipped the bracelet over her hand and hugged her one more time.

Stanley picked up the phone when Chloe left the den.

"Quinn, I want guards on Chloe and Danielle."

"Taken care of yesterday, Stan. As soon as I saw the download, I assigned guards for both of them. They'll be safe and not even know it."

"Thanks, Quinn."

"I married you guys. You're my closest friends. See you tomorrow at noon."

• • •

Danielle climbed into bed and Stanley hugged her tightly for a long time.

"You OK?" she finally asked after kissing him.

"Not at all."

"The meeting this morning?"

"It's worse than you can possibly imagine, honey…drugs and human trafficking being condoned and controlled by people in powerful positions. Norah Chase is just the tip of the iceberg. And what they did to A.W. – Pharmaceutical companies are involved in all this somehow; it's a rotten cauldron, honey."

"Talked to Richard a few days ago, right after Norah was rescued; told him about Amy Hamilton – that she's trying to blackmail you."

…that explains his battered face…

"Well, you want to hear the mother of all ironies?"

"Lay it on me."

"Your father was a stockholder in Coven Pharmaceuticals. So is Amy Hamilton. So are you; your father left his shares to you."

"Coven mixed up with all this?"

"Quinn says yes."

"I'll sell them all in the morning."

Danielle looked at her husband's tired face and moved closer, wrapping him in her arms and legs.

"I love you, Mister McMillen. We're going to be just fine."

"That's what our daughter told me."

"Then it's a done deal."

"She likes Basil Hayden's."

"I'm not even going to ask."

"She's an awful lot like you."

"I don't like Basil Hayden's."

CHAPTER 21

MAC & CHEESE

Doctor A.W. Blue sat in the upholstered green chair next to his hospital bed, wearing a blue suit. The nurses had taken up a collection amongst themselves and purchased it for him. A young nurse moved the over-the-bed table and positioned it in front of him. He smiled while the young blond ran a brush through his thin, gray hair. The old man looked up from a yellow legal pad, putting his pen down when Stanley and Drs. McCaferty and Smith walked in, followed by Richard and Quinn.

"Been making a list," A.W. said, looking up. His eyes sparkled with clarity.

"Here're the names I can recall," Doctor Blue continued. "Never truly knew the name of the fellow in charge of our addictions; just called him Wire-Rim. No matter; the contents of his cranium are splattered on the floor in St. Kitts, thanks to your wife," he said to Quinn.

"This is the committee that runs things. There's a fellow from Russia called Ivan. Have no idea if these are the real names, but this is what I remember. Raul is from Mexico, and there is a fellow they call John from England. Hector is from Brazil, and Simon is from South Africa, and there is Jimmy from China. Like I say, not sure if these are the true names. But this one I know for sure."

He pointed at the list scribbled on the yellow legal pad with his pen.

"This one I have met before in New Orleans. He is the CEO of Coven Pharmaceuticals. Gave a speech at a medical convention I attended."

He drew a circle around the name, ROBERT CASH.

"I'm sorry you've all been drawn into my abyss." The thin old man spoke with a soft, hoarse voice. He looked up at the men with eyes showing jaundiced sclera.

"Thank you for coming when you did for Norah. She is a sweet, sweet, innocent. I knew what they had planned for her."

Doctor Blue shook his head, almost quivering, involuntarily.

"I was not going to allow that. The ladies were not, either. They slipped me an occasional OxyContin or morphine tablet they had managed to hide under their tongues or regurgitate after Wire-Rim left the room. We called it Norah's escape plan. I planned to give Norah an overdose when that day came – the day we knew they were coming for her."

"We always knew." He paused and scratched the top of his head. "The princes would come on inspection tours, looking over the inventory."

"They would have killed you, A.W."

"Yes, quite likely. Rita is waiting; it'd be fine."

Stanley stood, watching an orderly dressed in green scrubs pushing a food cart down the hallway toward them.

"Who's the new orderly?" he asked the young nurse, who had just returned to replace a nearly empty IV bottle.

She turned and answered, "Never seen him before."

The orderly pushed the cart with a food tray past the first guard who lifted the stainless steel warming cover before nodding OK. The smiling orderly entered the room and placed the food tray on the over-the-bed table, pushing the yellow legal pad to the side. Stanley walked toward the young man, looking at his employee badge. The orderly removed the warming cover.

"My mind must be going; don't remember ordering mac & cheese, but this looks delicious."

The orderly turned and pushed his delivery cart toward the door.

The guard noticed, at the same instant Stanley did, an orderly pushing a cart with several food trays down the hall, stopping outside Doctor Blue's room.

"STOP…DON'T EAT!" the guard screamed at Doctor Blue. Buttering a slice of bread, Doctor Blue looked up, confused.

Richard Elmore Fortin stood.

The second orderly said, "Lunch is served; sorry for the delay"

The guard pushed the second orderly back into the hallway while blocking the doorway.

Every eye watched the first orderly's right hand grasp a pistol hidden in the small of his back, under his scrubs. They watched him twist around, seemingly in slow motion, extending his arm toward Doctor Blue.

The young blond nurse lurched toward the gun.

BANG! BANG! BANG!

The orderly's head jerked backward, his eyes dazed and mouth wide, before falling face down, arms outstretched. The gun slid on the tile floor until it stopped against Doctor Blue's right slipper.

Dressed completely in black, the muscular True Believer studied the man he had just shot three times then shook his head.

"Sorry I let him get past me, general," he said, bending over to pick up the shell casings.

"That was the bravest thing I've ever seen." Stanley put his arms around the young nurse.

"Nobody's shooting my patients," she replied, looking up at her boss. Then she smiled. "To be honest, Stanley, I'm kinda a chicken. That was just a reflex."

"A chicken's reflex is to flee danger, Mary."

She shrugged and smiled a tentative smile, quivering.

"Well," Doctor Blue said from his chair, "I guess they've found me."

"Yup," Quinn O'Malley replied. He looked at the plate of mac & cheese. "I put my money on cyanide."

"THIS IS EXACTLY WHAT I FEARED ALL ALONG, CHIEF STRAIT. I WARNED YOU!" Wyatt Tiffany's big Texas voice boomed down the hall.

Chief Strait, along with two officers, pushed past the orderly standing in the middle of the hallway holding a food tray, their side arms drawn, observing the True Believer holding a pistol. They walked into Doctor Blue's room and looked at the young man with curly brown hair, prone on the floor. The men watched the dark crimson circles growing around three holes in the young man's green scrub top.

"He's dead, Chief," Doctor Blue said.

"There you have it, Chief, there you have it, an innocent orderly shot in the back by one of your cowboys. I say, arrest that man, immediately!"

Ramona, the director of nursing, arrived, breathless.

"You hire this guy, Ramona?" Stanley asked.

"Never saw him before," she replied, lifting the man's Big Bay General ID badge from the bloody floor. "But, this is one of our ID badges."

"You know him, Wyatt?" Chief Strait demanded.

"I don't do the hiring."

"That's not what I asked."

"Never laid eyes on this poor boy before now."

"Whose gun?" Chief Strait asked, pointing at the pistol next to Doctor Blues' feet.

Everyone silently pointed at the dead orderly.

"Arrest that man," Wyatt Tiffany demanded. He pointed toward the True Believer standing in the doorway.

"Wyatt, your orderly came to this room with intent to commit a felony. He pulled a gun on a patient in your hospital. I think I'll have a conversation with the prosecutor. Not sure who needs to be arrested here."

Wyatt Tiffany uttered, "Stupid Yankees," and walked past the True Believer, still holding his pistol.

He bumped the guard with his shoulder as he passed by.

"Pay no heed, Mack," Quinn said to his guard.

Mack smiled and holstered his pistol.

Wyatt Tiffany turned ten feet from the door and shouted, pointing at Chief Strait, "Well Larry, we'll see what my friend Ronald Berlinski down to the Marshall's Service has to say on this particular misfortune."

He stomped away toward his office.

Quinn moved close to Chief Strait. "Larry, have them draw blood samples; check this guy for narcotics and such."

"I'm thinking the same thing, Quinn."

"And," Quinn said while placing the stainless steel cover over the mac & cheese, "take this with you. Analyze it for poisons."

"Anyone want to be my official taster?"

Every head turned to see Doctor Blue, leaning forward in his chair; playing with his fork. His tired face wrinkled into a sardonic smile.

CHAPTER 22

THE AGONY

Their children had left for school. Katie and Doug watched their four grade-schoolers walking away from the parsonage on the sidewalk, teasing each other and laughing.

"They have brought us more joy than I could have imagined," Katie said.

"I'm happy we were able to adopt them," Doug replied.

"What are your plans today?" Katie asked Doug.

"Clean the garage and tune-up the lawn mower and rototiller. Get stuff ready for spring. How 'bout you?"

"Going to meet Belvia at 10:00, go to the hospital and get Norah. She's being discharged today. Then, I think we'll go shopping at Target. They left most of their clothes in Key West."

Doug hugged his wife.

"You're one special lady. I love you."

"Love you, too. Want me to drop off some lunch?"

"Naw, I'll get a bowl of chili at Poor Joe's."

"OK. I'll be home around 4:00."

And she kissed him.

• • •

The spark plug came out of the lawn mower without hesitation, and the oil plug, too. Within twenty minutes, Doug had the green machine running top notch. The older rototiller refused to give up its spark plug. He could not find a plug wrench to fit exactly, and when the crescent wrench slipped, the white porcelain top broke.

"Well, that's just terrific," he muttered, using an old oil rag to wipe away some blood oozing from his knuckles.

He rubbed at his dizzy eyes.

...the agony, reminiscent of the time Tommy Hesselgeffer accidently kicked him in the testicles during recess, collapsing from the monkey bars with the air no longer in his lungs, gasping like his pet goldfish, Elmer, who had jumped out of the fish bowl when the bowl had been filled too full, thrashing about on the floor, leaving a little wet trail in the dust, his mouth opening and closing...

Blackness interrupted by brilliant flashes. His pacing defibrillator shocking him repeatedly with sequentially stronger and stronger shocks, diagnosing and treating the spontaneous ventricular fibrillation, the very reason Doctor McCaferty had implanted it in the first place.

All blackness.

One last brilliant flash before darkness again.

Doug's body lay slumped over the rototiller.

●●●

She appeared through the shroud. Janet Sue reached for his hand and when they touched, the darkness disappeared. In a long line stood his buddies who had died during the battle of Operation Hump. They saluted just briefly before breaking into happy cheers, and Norma Bouvier came close, and so, too, did Charley Johnson, hugging him. She led Doug past them all and toward Him. And when they touched, all the sounds around them became colors, and there was no sadness whatsoever, just love.

"Hi honey. I'm home," Katie said from the kitchen.

She walked around the house looking and then through the side door to the garage.

CHAPTER 23

AULD LANG SYNE

They all gathered – as they had for many years, except when Poor Joe's closed during the time eight-year-old Chloe lay near death with influenza – on Wednesday night to play poker. With reverence, they walked past Doug's chair, his jacket draped from the back and his Baltimore Orioles baseball cap on the table in front of the chair. An unopened deck of playing cards, wrapped in cellophane, leaned against the cap.

The popcorn machine made the usual pop-pop-popping sounds, and the Magnavox television above the bar played on with the sound off, the weather girl excitedly pointing to a deep low pressure area over Iowa.

"We sat right over there," Wendell said, pointing toward a booth. "Stanley told me that he heard Doug was living in a tent along the river, just above the dam, and winter was coming, so I looked him up, and we talked right over there. Told him that in a few months the snow would be knee deep and that he should join us – that I bet Timothy would rent him a room upstairs. We sat right over there and ate Dora's spicy clam chowder."

"That's the night I offered Doug a job. Told him I needed a bouncer and he asked, 'Why me?' and I told him because he had no fear in him," Timothy said.

"He told us that night about November 8, 1965, Operation Hump, when his buddies were ambushed and slaughtered, the afternoon an angel floated into his turret. She sat beside him in the Green Dragon and sang a song to him," Wendell added.

"Him and his dog, Malcolm, almost inseparable. Not a pair to be trifled with, right Machete?" Stanley interjected.

Machete smiled.

"I just needed to be with my baby sister."

"What you did, Machete, was kidnap little Chloe McMillen. Doug and Malcolm tracked you all the way across town and found you in a vacant house," Wendell said.

"Yes, that's true, amigo."

Pete pointed to the buckshot holes in the hardwood floor.

"I'll never forget the night of Norma's retirement party when those bikers from New York City barged in."

"I told them it was a private party," Timothy said with a little smile.

"When the big bearded biker hit your mom, Timothy, that's when all hell busted loose. And then BOOM...BOOM from the stairs," Pete continued. "There stood Doug with a 12 gauge pump. The fight ended."

"It must have been ten years ago, or so, when I told Doug he had to stop drinking, not another drop, that his heart had been weakened from all the alcohol and that he would die if he continued to drink. He told me he didn't care, and I said that was selfish; what about his friends who love him? He never had another drop. I hoped the pacing defibrillator would keep this from happening," Doctor McCaferty said.

"Who would have ever dreamed that Doug would end up marrying a beautiful young lady like Katie?" Wayne said.

"It was always my dream, Wayne, and it came true."

They turned to see Katie walking through the front door with her children. Danielle and Chloe walked with them, followed by Quinn and Debra.

"I met Doug at this very table," Katie continued. "I sat down right there and told all you guys I liked poker and then won every hand the rest of the evening. Doug kept staring at me and finally asked me, 'Are you married?' and I said, 'No, how about you?' That's how we met. My parents, you guys will remember, were not happy with me, nor was my old boyfriend who made a ruckus during one Sunday service from the balcony."

"You have no idea how much that upset Doug or what he had planned for him," Timothy said.

"Oh, trust me, I knew. Thank God, Chief Strait intervened and encouraged him to go back to New York."

"So you're not going to have a funeral?" Wendell asked.

"He hated funerals. I promised him," Katie replied. "This is his favorite place on earth, and Wednesday poker night his favorite evening of the week. I thought we could all just come here and be close to him," she said, pointing at his chair, "and remember him as the kind and truly gentle person who, when he saw wrong, tried to make it better and never intentionally hurt anyone. I am going to miss him very much."

Katie slid Doug's chair away from the table and sat down. She put Doug's ball cap on, and smiled. "He never washed this, you know."

"I remember sitting on Machete's lap, and he was rocking me, and then I remember being under Doug's arm, looking at all the people on the sidewalk watching us go by. That's all I remember from that time, that you were kind, Machete, and that Doug was brave. Over all the years since that day, you have both been precious to me," Chloe said, standing next to her mother. "This is the first time I've lost someone I love, and my heart feels like a stone inside."

"Every New Year he would cry when 'Auld Lang Syne' came on at midnight, and then he would wipe away the tears and laugh at himself," Katie said.

Carla stood and walked over to the old upright piano and began to play.

Every person inside Poor Joe's sang.

"Should auld acquaintance be forgot
And never brought to mind?
Should auld acquaintance be forgot,
And days of o'lang syne!
For auld lang syne, my dear
For auld lang syne,
We'll take a cup o' kindness yet
For auld lang syne!"

● ● ●

Katie reached behind her and lifted Doug's jacket from the chair back.

They watched from the poker table; they watched from the booths and the round tables. Katie rolled the jacket into a pillow. They all watched as she placed it on the poker table and snuggled her face deep into the pillow and inhaled deeply.

CHAPTER 24

MOSES FROM GUADELOUPE

" **M**y name be Moses."

Timothy turned from the chili pot, looking at a dark-skinned young lady with blue eyes, her arm outstretched, speaking with a Caribbean accent.

He grinned and shook her hand.

"Never met a Moses before today. What's your last name, Moses?"

"Just Moses. De parish priest found me in da wicker basket on de church steps and named me Moses before de nuns told him I be a baby girl. De name stuck."

"Where you from?"

"Guadeloupe. Jen at your city's Cuban restaurant don't need no help; she's all set; says your cook, Dorothy, left wid Fidel Castro to Cuba and all you serve now be chili and hot dogs and popcorn. She say you could use plenty of help."

"Dora, her name is Dora. She married Fidel four years ago. This place hasn't been quite the same since she left."

"Oh."

"You cook?"

"I be a really good cook. You like Caribbean and French?"

"We're a little simpler, Moses. Burgers and soups…and the guys love cinnamon rolls for breakfast."

"I make de best breakfast rolls!"

Moses' eyes twinkled with excitement.

"I make delicious cinnamon nut rolls, apple croissants, chocolate almond croissants, coconut raspberry croissants, pear almond croissants…"

She took a breath.

Timothy grinned.

…she'll brighten this place…

"…and I make delicious eggs Benedict, ham and cheese omelets, and crêpes."

"When can you start?"

"Now be good; and for de evenings I make hot roast beef baguettes and grilled ham and cheese…and key lime coconut crepes for your delicious desserts."

Timothy bent down to her level, whispering, "You a citizen of the United States or have a green card?"

"No mister."

"Call me Timothy. I know a fellow who can help you in that department."

"Dat be wonderful."

"Where are you staying?"

"What's dat mean?"

"Where are you living?"

"In my Chevrolet."

"There's a vacant room," Timothy pointed up the stairs, "that you can use; part of your salary."

"Thank you."

"Let's take a look at the kitchen and make a list of groceries you'll need, Moses."

●●●

Quinn held a black thumb drive between his thumb and forefinger, waving it at eye level, for everyone to see.

"It took a German supercomputer to decipher the encryption on this."

He sat facing the front entrance, as was his habit, watching people enter and leave Poor Joe's. Richard sat opposite, with Victor and Rose on either side.

"On this chip are the names of governors, congressmen, doctors, princes, pharmaceutical company CEOs, drug reps, pharmacists, drug lords, casino owners, and hospital administrators in the U.S., England, France, Japan, China, Russia, Brazil, Mexico, and South Africa. *The Company* is a multifaceted business dealing in legal drugs furnished to hospitals, doctors' offices, pain clinics, street distribution, and the sex trade; human trafficking where girls are purchased as wives, and for prostitution."

Quinn leaned to his left, handing the list to Rose. She read the names of several casinos and shook her head.

Clack…click…click…clack…the sound of Amy Hamilton's stilettos against Poor Joe's oak floor.

"Hi, Tim!" she exclaimed, sitting on a bar stool and examining her hair in the mirror.

"Hi, Amy, how you been?"

"Never better. Busy. Heard anything from Stan?"

"Don't look right now, Richard," Quinn said, "but Amy Hamilton just walked in; talking to Timothy."

"He's been in, seems fine, why?"

"Just wondering. Had an appointment with him. He cancelled," Amy replied with a smirk.

"Well, look what the cat dragged in," Richard muttered.

Amy felt his presence behind her before he said the first word. She looked away from Timothy and at the mirror's reflection then swiveled on the bar stool. Looking up, she sucked in a deep involuntary breath. Richard Elmore Fortin's face stared at her, the glass eye she remembered from the rearview mirror now twelve inches from her face, not blinking.

She turned her face back toward Timothy. He shrugged.

"We have a conversation to finish," Richard said.

"WHAT THE HELL'RE YOU DOING OUT OF JAIL?" she yelled, climbing from her bar stool. "I'm leaving."

"Nope, you're not," Richard said. "You're even dirtier than I thought. Just wanted to talk to you about Stanley when we met in Tennessee, but the picture has changed a bit. Come over here," He grasped Amy firmly by the arm while walking toward the southwest table.

"Tim, call the police; I'm being assaulted."

"My recommendation is go with him, Amy."

"You, too?" she snapped, looking back.

"I want you to meet my friends," Richard said, pulling a fifth chair to the table while holding her arm. "They have several questions for you."

"You have bad people in Big Bay, as we do in Guadeloupe," Moses whispered to Timothy.

"What?"

Moses pointed toward Amy Hamilton.

"She be a bad one. I feel her badness. I'm a Rastafarian."

Timothy smiled. "Mind if I give you a hug?"

"Do you have a wife?"

"Carla would approve," Timothy replied.

"Welcome to Poor Joe's."

"Thank you."

"No pot smoking in the bar, Moses."

Moses' blue eyes smiled.

CHAPTER 25

IT IS A SIN

"I am not a religious man. I have watched religion destroy countries and hurt friends. Greedy people and power mongers hold their righteous banners high, finding excerpts from their scriptures to justify murders and horrendous acts beyond civilized thought. I have seen precious little children mistreated, confused, and bewildered. The look in their eyes haunts me. I have been witness to evil that makes me nauseated; in the name of this religion or that, it doesn't seem to matter. I believe in God. Richard, here, has met him and says he's a nice guy, a loving fellow; I believe Richard."

Quinn spoke without blinking, directly at Amy.

"So my rules are not complicated by dogma. I know evil when I see it. It is a sin to hurt children and ruin their innocence. It is a sin to promote drugs destroying souls and to hold captive struggling humans. It is a sin to kidnap young ladies, forcing them to sacrifice their bodies for the pleasure of rotten selfish men, stealing from them their childhood dreams of falling in love and being close to a man. It is a sin to kill hopes and dreams."

Quinn's eyes flashed with anger, still without blinking.

"There is a word that says it all: unconscionable. Hadn't thought of that word for a long time until I heard it recently. I think failure to protect the innocent ones is unconscionable." Quinn continued, "When I finally pass over and join my friends, I will not be ashamed. I will reach for God's hand and say thank you. Until then, I will endeavor to prevent people like you from hurting one more person."

"Who are you?" Amy's voice trembled a little.

"My name is Quinn O'Malley."

…shit…

"That name supposed to mean something to me? Like I should bend down and pay homage?" Amy shot back.

Quinn played with the black thumb drive then held it toward Amy.

"Got this in St. Kitts. Has your name on it, along with others, including Robert Cash. You're going to take us to Robert Cash."

"I don't know a Robert Cash."

"I think you know him very well, Amy. And you know how to contact him, which is exactly what you're going to do."

"What I'm going to do is leave here right now and drive to the police station and file a report."

"How'd that work out for you in Tennessee?" Richard asked.

She stared back. "Just how did you get out of jail?"

"Grandpa bailed me out. Now you can either tell us everything we want to know or we take a field trip, and then you tell us everything we want to know," Richard said.

"Go to hell."

"Well, actually, it will be a much more pleasant trip," Quinn replied, putting the thumb drive in his shirt pocket. "Sodium Pentothal. I'm sure you're familiar, given your chosen profession."

"CALL THE POLICE!" Amy screamed at Timothy, standing behind the bar. He turned his back and winked at Moses.

Chapter 26

Snake Eyes

"Daddy, Mister Tiffany is on the phone," Chloe shouted from the living room.

Stanley looked at Chloe from his wicker chair on the deck under a gas heater. Slowly, he walked to the phone.

"Hello."

"Stanley, I'm sitting here in my office contemplating things. Feel we've gotten off on a patch of rough road, young man. I want you to come down to my office and discuss things."

"It's nine fifteen."

"Well, hell, man, what's time got to do with a little reconciliation and fence mending. You come on down here."

"Thank you, I'm declining."

"Now, Stanley, some things need to be said face-to-face. You come down from your hilltop and meet with me, immediately."

"No, sir, I think not."

"If that is your answer, I'm obliged to insist you do the proper thing and tender your resignation. I want only team players on my management staff, showing a good example for our employees."

"Not a problem; I have opportunities elsewhere."

"My influence reaches far, Stanley. I'll do my best to see you are working in a Burger King."

"I haven't needed to work for several years. And I doubt your arm of influence reaches where Danielle and I would go. But, I'll tell you what, I'll meet you in the corner booth at Poor Joe's next to the popcorn machine. Meet you there in fifteen minutes; even buy you a beer."

"I'll see you in fifteen minutes. I have a friend you should meet."

...thought so...

Stanley called Poor Joe's.

"Poor Joe's. Joe's dead, Timothy here."

"That should be good for business," Stanley replied.

"What's up, Stan?"

"Wyatt Tiffany is meeting me in the corner booth fifteen minutes from now. Think he's not alone. Timothy, given what Quinn discovered on the thumb drives, this could be trouble."

Timothy reached under the counter and picked up his pistol. He put it in his left pocket.

"Richard and Quinn left two days ago. I'll have Pete and Wayne downstairs with me. We'll keep an eye on things."

"Ask Machete to sit in the booth; have him sitting there when Tiffany arrives. I'll arrive a little late."

"Honey," Danielle said, listening from the living room, "don't go."

"Can't let Tiffany intimidate me. The guys will be there. It'll be fine. Besides, Machete will be there as my advisor."

He squeezed Danielle particularly tightly. She could feel his biceps trembling.

Chloe walked out from her bedroom. She and Danielle listened to Stanley drive down the hill. When the sound faded away completely, she said to her mom, "Dad really is a hero."

"He really is, honey."

●●●

Big Wyatt Tiffany strode through Poor Joe's front door at nine thirty, following a small man with a shaved, shiny scalp. They turned left and approached the designated booth.

"Excuse me there, little blind man, we have a business meeting in this reserved booth."

"My name is Machete."

"Well then, Machete, like I say, we have this booth reserved."

Machete stroked Little Miss, his left hand repeatedly going down her back. Little Miss sat next to him, looking up at the Texan's groin area with her brown eyes.

The little shiny headed man fidgeted, glancing about with eyes that reminded Timothy of a snake looking for prey. He focused on Pete and Wayne sitting at the round southwest table for a few seconds and squinted.

Timothy stood behind the bar, next to the cash register, his left hand pushed into his pants pocket.

Stanley walked in.

"Our designated booth has been usurped by a little blind man and his dog, Stanley. I say let's go back to my office."

The shiny headed man nodded in agreement.

"Hi, my name is Stanley McMillen." Stanley extended his right hand.

"Vladimir Khrushchev, advisor to Mister Tiffany."

Stanley grinned while they shook hands. "Meet Machete Juarez, advisor to Stanley McMillen."

Machete looked up at Vladimir with his blind eyes.

"Mister Khrushchev worked as counsel for several concerns in Russia before moving to the United States and becoming a U.S. citizen," Wyatt Tiffany said, looking down at Machete.

"Mister Juarez worked in the employ of several concerns in Mexico City before moving to Big Bay and becoming a citizen," Stanley retorted. "I trust him with my life."

Wyatt Tiffany's head jerked just a little.

"You called this meeting; let's sit down and get started. Want a beer or something?"

Wyatt Tiffany squeezed into the booth. Vladimir stood. Machete stood to let Stanley slide in, then sat next to Little Miss.

"Nothing for me," Wyatt said.

"I'll have what Stanley's having," Machete said in the direction of the bar. Timothy walked to the booth with two Basil Hayden's on the rocks.

"Sure you don't want a little vodka, Vladimir?" Timothy said, staring directly into the snake eyes.

"I'm listening," Stanley said after a long sip.

"I apologize for any misunderstandings we may have, Stanley, on this pain clinic business. Vladimir and I have worked on this project for several years now, setting up clinics around this great nation of ours, providing relief for those who have served our nation in times of war and have returned home with grievous pains. We have now…what? Vladimir…I think twelve clinics running or about to open. It warms our hearts to be of assistance. That little disagreement we had during the department head meeting involved costs, Stanley. I am…Vladimir here…we're numbers people, trying to provide relief and not go bust doing it."

"Genuine patriots," Stanley replied. "Vladimir, how well do you know Amy Hamilton?"

"That name is not familiar to me."

Machete spoke softly. "Miss Hamilton is currently in the company of Quinn O'Malley and Richard Elmore Fortin. I think she will tell a very different story, amigos, about your businesses."

Vladimir stiffened. "I have no idea who those people you mention are or why they are of my concern."

"You make me think of a man I once knew in Mexico City by the name of Cesar Veracruz – a very evil, selfish man with much power; so much power, he thought himself invincible. He died one night after visiting his favorite brothel. Someone cut the brake lines to his Mercedes Benz and he died that night. His evil nephews took over the drug business; they all died one dark night when a radioactive meteorite landed on their compound. The news shocked my home country. No one misses them now."

"Is that a thinly veiled threat there, little blind man?" Wyatt Tiffany growled.

"That is a true story. You can look it up, *muy cierto.*"

"Robhd!" Vladimir muttered to himself.

"Just so you understand, we know the true purpose of the pain clinics you guys are sponsoring and staffing around the country, Wyatt," Stanley said. "And we are going to know much more very soon. And, you should know, Chief Strait has sent the lunch that was served to Doctor Blue to the state police crime lab for analysis."

"Now why would that be of my concern, what your Chief Barney does with a meal served by an obviously deranged young man, a terrorist of sorts?"

Stanley smiled.

"Judge Linsenmayer is eagerly awaiting the results, too," Stanley continued, watching Vladimir's eyes flit around the room and Wyatt scratching his big chin.

"Something about a warrant waiting to be signed."

Vladimir Khrushchev leaned over the table and stared into Stanley's face.

"Be sure to say hello to your wife." He turned to leave and stopped. "And, to your daughter…Chloe isn't it?"

Chapter 27

The Color Of Darkness

They left, Wyatt Tiffany stomping on the hard old floors through the front door, slamming the screen door open so hard one hinge broke, leaving the door dangling from the lone top attachment. Vladimir had walked out backward, following the big Texan, watching while he walked.

The big Texan face reappeared through the open door just for an instant. "By the way, you're fired. I'll have your personal belongings boxed up and ready for your retrieval on Monday."

"Can he fire you, just like that?" Wayne asked.

"That he can, Wayne, that he can."

Stanley reached into his jacket pocket and grabbed the triangular yellow Comstat phone. He noticed his index finger trembled while he punched in a sequence of numbers and letters from memory, ending with a capital Q.

Machete listened to Stanley's voice, now steely.

"What, Stanley?"

"I know you're occupied, Quinn. I need help."

"What?"

"You know a Vladimir Khrushchev?"

"Head of cartel drug distribution based in Chicago. His name comes up on both thumb drives. Why?"

"Had a meeting with Wyatt Tiffany. Vladimir came with him. Wyatt called him his advisor."

Stanley paused and took two deep breaths.

"Vladimir just threatened Danielle and Chloe."

Stanley listened to Quinn rub his beard.

"I'll send my plane tonight. You guys need to get out of the country."

"Thanks, Quinn."

"Get to the private hangar. The plane will be there at three."

"Where to?"

"I'll let you know. Just be at the hangar at three."

Stanley pushed the off button and looked up. Timothy, Pete, and Wayne stood around the booth, listening.

"Moses, you turn things off and close up," Timothy shouted toward the kitchen.

"We escort Stanley home and stay with the McMillens until they're on Quinn's plane," Timothy continued, resorting to his Green Beret instincts. "Machete, you stay here with Moses and load your shotgun with buckshot. Get your sidearms. Let's go. Leave your car here, Stanley; ride with us."

Stanley called Danielle.

"Get packed; Quinn has a plane coming for us."

Her husband's voice felt cold and angry.

"Lock the doors until I get home, and pack just enough to get by. I'll explain. Put Chloe on."

"Hi, Daddy."

"We have to leave on Uncle Quinn's plane tonight. Pack just enough for a couple of days. I'll explain when I get home. Do not open the door for anyone."

"Wow, dad, what'd you do?"

"I'll explain. Get packing."

Stanley phoned Chief Strait.

"Larry, would you have a squad car outside our place. Danielle and Chloe are in danger; we're leaving on Quinn's plane tonight. I'll explain more when we're in the air."

"I'll drive up the hill and do it myself, Stan."

"Thanks. Quinn has a couple of fellows shadowing them, but I'd feel even better with a patrol car outside our front door."

"State Police finished their evaluation on A.W.'s lunch. Quinn was right…cyanide."

"These are bad people, Larry. Be careful."

"I've got my bullet polished."

"You've heard, huh?"

"Wyatt's been calling me Barney all over town. Get going, Stan. We'll take care of business, just get going."

On the drive up the hill, Stanley called Doctor McCaferty.

"Jack, my family has been threatened by Tiffany's henchman, name of Vladimir. Quinn's sending his plane to fly us out of town. Be careful around Tiffany. He just fired me."

"Quinn called me after you called him; just finished. I'm on my way to the hospital right now. He wants A.W. on the plane."

"What a stinking mess. You be careful, Jack."

"Quinn's having the guards travel with us; we'll be fine."

"Thanks, Jack."

"Of course."

● ● ●

Moses cleaned the grills with a pumice stone, finishing by wiping the surfaces with lard. Drying her hands on a bar towel, she walked quietly to Machete, sitting next to Little Miss at the far end of the bar, in the darkness. He looked in her direction as she approached.

"You hear everything," she said, sitting next to him.

"Yes."

"How do you aim de shotgun?"

"Little Miss tells me."

"I could not shoot another person. I will help Little Miss, if you like."

"Thank you. I hope they do not come back."

"Dey be surrounded wit de darkness," Moses said, putting her left hand on Machete's arm.

He smiled. "You could see it, too?"

"Yes, very dark."

"I can see the color of darkness," Machete replied, "and I hate it."

"I will sit here wit you tonight 'til our men get back."

"I would like that."

• • •

At 3:15 a.m. the city of Big Bay awakened; windows vibrated, the bottles of booze behind the bar at Poor Joe's rattled against the mirror, and dogs all around the city, inside and out, howled and barked into the darkness.

The sleek white Gulfstream S-21's three jet engines roared mightily, thrusting the needle-nosed jet down the short Big Bay runway and up over the city, climbing steeply to 60,000 feet, and then leveling off, traveling at Mach 2.

Jack McCaferty stood on the tarmac next to the True Believer named Mark, looking up into the dark sky, listening to the sound growing distant.

• • •

Timothy walked up the steps and looked at the dangling screen door. He opened the main door just a crack and yelled, "Don't shoot, Machete, we're back!"

Timothy, Pete, and Wayne walked in. Sitting in the shadows, they saw Machete holding a shotgun with his left hand and holding Moses' hand with his other. Little Miss sat in front of Machete. Her tail swished back and forth on the floor.

"This has been one strange night," Wayne said.

CHAPTER 28

A PERFECT CLONE

W yatt Tiffany strutted into the hospital's large conference room and pulled the microphone from the podium stand. He walked around on the stage in front of the packed room, his eyes going from person to person, measuring the attitudes from the eyes glaring at him.

"I have a bit of sad news," he started, walking off the stage and down the center aisle and then returning to the front. "I'm sure by now you know Stanley McMillen is no longer employed at Big Bay General. I like Stanley, but we had a little disagreement on management styles and Stanley felt it best to resign."

"Yeah, Stanley is honest," came from deep in the crowd.

"At any rate, time marches on," Mister Tiffany continued. "As much as we will all miss Stanley, time marches on. I have asked Miss Tewsley in HR to begin a search for a new critical care director. I will keep you informed on my progress. On a brighter note, I am happy to announce an across-the-board five-percent raise in all your paychecks. Big Bay General is having a banner year. Thank you all for your hard work."

He was pushing the microphone back into the podium holder when he spotted Chief Strait walking through the side door in the company of two state policemen and one deputy. Wyatt Tiffany did not move, standing beside the podium, glaring at the men approaching him.

"Wyatt Tiffany, you are under arrest," Chief Strait said.

"On what charges?"

"Conspiracy to commit murder."

"Bullshit."

"Please place your hands behind your back," the bigger of the two big state policeman said.

Timid clapping started somewhere in the back of the conference room and then became raucous cheering.

"Now just a pea-picking minute here; this is a mistake, a humongous error," Tiffany barked.

"We have proof that you ordered human resources to make an ID badge for the man posing as an orderly. We have a warrant, signed by Judge Linsenmayer."

"Liars! My word against hers. No such thing ever happened," he said, glaring at Miss Tewsley.

Ramona, the director of nursing, leaned close to Miss Tewsley, and whispered, "The fat fool doesn't know we have video surveillance in ER, peds, pharmacy, and HR; damn him."

"I'm scared," Miss Tewsley answered.

"Don't be. The video will do the talking."

Ramona hesitated then said, "And, you have friends you don't even know."

The cheers grew loud when Wyatt Tiffany, his hands cuffed behind his back, marched out of the room with defiance flashing in his eyes.

• • •

The flight from Big Bay to Nueva Gerona on the Isle of Youth, Cuba, took seventy minutes. On the flight down, Stanley and Danielle introduced Chloe to A.W. Blue. They told her about the years they all worked together at Big Bay General. Doctor Blue told Chloe the story of running off to Key West with his office nurse, and his reason why. He told her about the years Rita and he had worked together on Cayo Coco, Cuba, and how devastating her death had been to him – how absolutely crushingly alone he felt – and that he would take his fishing boat out to talk to Rita almost every evening because they always watched the sunset together when she was alive.

"That's where I first met you, you know, on the Cayo Coco beach at sunset."

Chloe looked slightly puzzled and glanced at her mother.

"Your uncle Quinn took your parents to Cayo Coco for their honeymoon."

The old man chuckled a little while he took Chloe's hand in his wrinkled hand, his fingers deformed by arthritis.

"Your mom was pregnant and I knew it, even though they never said. We were sitting on beach chairs and a big wave rolled right over her and her top washed up and I saw her belly. You were just getting started and look at you now, a perfect clone of your mom."

"Mom says I think like my dad."

"Best of both. I like the way your daddy thinks."

"What happened next? Mom said you disappeared for ten years."

A.W. looked at Stanley and Danielle. Stanley nodded yes.

"I was kidnapped and made to work in a very evil place."

"What kind of evil place?"

Stanley nodded again.

"A place where young ladies were brought to be sold to rich men for pleasure."

Chloe stared at her mother's face and then back to Doctor Blue's, then back.

"That must have been awful!"

"It was hell, Chloe. But now I know why I was put in that place."

"Why?"

Stanley nodded again.

"To save Norah Chase. They brought her there and I looked after her."

"Oh, I didn't know that happened to Norah. Poor Norah!"

"It's not too early to learn, Chloe, that when you're looking at a person, there is much you don't know. Do not assume until you know the truth. Often the truth is hidden very deep. Anyway, your Uncle Quinn and Richard Elmore Fortin came to our rescue. Things are fine now."

Stanley and Danielle watched their daughter lovingly run her hand down the old man's cheek and lean close to him.

"I'm just a kid," Chloe said, looking directly at A.W., "but I know we wouldn't be on Uncle Quinn's plane headed someplace in the middle of the night if everything was alright."

She twisted around to face her father.

"Where are we going, anyway?"

Stanley opened the note the pilot had handed to him when they boarded. He handed it to his daughter.

"Nueva Gerona."

Chloe leaned back and grinned.

"I love that place. You're going to love it, Doctor Blue."

A.W. smiled at her innocent enthusiasm.

CHAPTER 29

ONE OF SEVEN

The 8,000 foot Rafael Cabrera Airport runway glowed a soft yellow, fully illuminated the entire length. They circled twice while the pilots communicated to the control tower and then the prototype Gulfstream landed in Nueva Gerona. The plane coasted to a stop next to an idling, black Chaika limousine.

Chloe exited the plane first. She no sooner stepped on the tarmac than the passenger doors of the limousine opened and Fidel Castro stepped out with his wife Dora.

Chloe ran.

Fidel handed his cane to Dora, extending both arms toward the gleeful teenager.

"I'm so happy that you're here," Chloe said in Spanish, snuggling close to the president of Cuba.

"You are even more beautiful, Chloe Norma, than when I last saw you. How old would you be, sixteen?"

"I am next week!"

"There will be a glorious party; I'll see to it."

Stanley and Danielle approached with Doctor Blue in a wheelchair being pushed by Stanley.

Fidel looked at his old friend and shrugged, shaking his head.

"The years are beating us up, A.W."

"That they are, Mister President. You look like a tired mule," Doctor Blue continued in Spanish, gently shaking his old friend's hand.

Then Fidel Castro, holding his wife's hand, turned and looked at Stanley and Danielle.

"O'Malley told me. You will be quite safe here, as you know. My place is yours for as long as necessary."

He smiled. "Perhaps one of these times I will convince you to stay. Doctor Gonzales would love that."

He shook hands with Stanley and hugged Danielle. Dora hugged Stanley and Danielle, then Chloe.

"I can't believe how much you and your mother look alike the older you get, honey!" Dora said to Chloe.

"I was saddened to hear that Doug died recently. I planned on traveling to his funeral then learned Katie decided not to have one," Fidel said.

"We held a memorial for him on poker night at Poor Joe's. Katie explained how Doug hated funerals and she had promised him when they got married," Danielle said.

Fidel smiled. "That sounds like Doug. I would have loved that. Your Poor Joe's is a very special place in my heart."

"Everyone cried when Katie made a pillow with Doug's jacket and buried her face into it. That night my heart felt like a broken stone," Chloe said.

"How's Katie now?" Dora asked, walking back toward the limo. Just then, a second limo arrived, being escorted by two armed Jeeps.

"She's devastated, Dora. She told me last Sunday that she thought she had prepared herself for his dying, knowing about his bad heart and that he was so much older. But it's still kinda crushed her, and the children, too."

Fidel stopped walking. They all stopped, looking at him.

"I want her telephone number. I will call her later today, and invite her to come visit. It will do her heart good. Do you have it, Danielle?"

"I'll send it to your cell phone," Chloe said in Spanish, with a grin. "I bet I'm the only teenager with your cell phone number!"

"You are one of seven people in the world."

"What are you doing up at 4:30 in the morning, Fidel?" Stanley asked.

The old man put his arm on Stanley's shoulder while they walked toward the cars.

"You were at my side when my heart fibrillated. You never left when Major Alvarez Prieto and his band of assassins came to kill me in Cardenas. I will never forget that night – you sitting on that chair with a little black six-shooter."

Stanley grinned.

"I remember your gun was shinier than mine."

"Let's have an early breakfast. I called Lina already. She will have *café con leche* ready when we arrive. You ride with us, A.W.," Fidel Castro said.

"Lina? I thought Richard had concerns about her, the last time we were here," Stanley asked.

Fidel smiled. "Richard has a way of working out problems." He handed his cane to the driver and slid into the back seat.

"He will arrive here tomorrow, I think."

CHAPTER 30

"THESE NEED ELIMINATED"

The Scarab racing boat idled, moving slowly up the Suriname River, finally stopping at the Fort Willoughby marina in Paramaribo, Suriname. The boat had traveled all night from Panama through calm seas.

Robert Cash climbed the red masonry steps while looking at the guards holding automatic weapons on the ground level and second story porches of the white wooden caretaker's residence. The committee waited inside.

"We have problems, Robert," Ivan Brezhnev said.

"Fill me in." Robert took his seat at the head of the table.

"The St. Kitts invasion has greatly compromised our operations. Three computers with information detailing our contacts were taken. They cracked the wall safe – held very sensitive papers – and two thumb drives with detailed information on each of our operations."

"I thought that safe was impenetrable," John Hall from England said, sarcastically.

"The thumb drives will be useless to them," Simon Zuma from South Africa commented. "They will not break the encryption."

"They already have," Ivan replied.

Everyone stared at the Russian.

He continued, "Vladimir informed me that Quinn O'Malley has the information from the thumb drives, that he has taken Amy Hamilton away for interrogation, that Wyatt Tiffany has been arrested, and that our efforts to neutralize Doctor Blue have been unsuccessful."

Robert Cash rubbed his beard. His blue eyes glared.

"Where are Amy Hamilton and Doctor Blue now?"

"We don't know. Vladimir said they disappeared," Ivan replied.

"How about all the women from the St. Kitts clinic? They could be used as witnesses; any idea where they might be?" Robert Cash asked with a sarcastic tone.

"Vanished. The FBI put them into some sort of witness protection thing. They're gone," Ivan answered. "Vladimir said they've vanished."

"How about the million-dollar girl we sold to Prince Asiad, the one from Key West?"

"They moved back to that city called Big Bay. She's in Big Bay."

Robert Cash cupped his hands and blew in them, like they felt cold.

"Well," he said, "our best laid plans have gone to hell. All our backup plans are on those thumb drives."

He motioned for a guard. "I need some rum."

"The first thing, we need to eliminate as many problems as we can, immediately."

He sipped a tumbler filled with dark rum.

"These problems need eliminated: Quinn O'Malley – find him, get the thumb drives, and eliminate him. And eliminate that Richard Elmore Fortin along with that girl in Big Bay. Someone find where Doctor Blue disappeared to, and finish the job. Dammit!

"And eliminate that fat Texan before he blabs to save his skin."

"What about Amy Hamilton?" Ivan asked.

"Her, too."

He took another sip of rum.

"And each of you contact your respective public officials and remind them we still have the virus.

"We meet back here in one week. I expect good news," Robert said, lifting the tumbler. He emptied it.

CHAPTER 31

AS LONG AS IT TAKES

Katie sat in the rectory office, staring at a picture of Doug and her standing on the beach, facing each other, her arms on his shoulders, with the orange setting sun above their heads.

When she wiped the tears from the top page of next Sunday's sermon, the blue ink smeared.

Ring…ring…ring…ring…ring…

She looked at her cell phone, trying to identify the caller and then shrugged and picked it up.

"Hello?"

"Katherine, this is Fidel Castro. We met at Poor Joe's during the Gonzales' wedding reception."

Katie held the phone out and looked at the calling number again.

"Hello, Mister President."

"If you call me Fidel, I will not call you Reverend."

Katie laughed. "Deal."

"I am sorry your husband has died. I liked Doug very much; admired his bravery and honesty. I watched the two of you during my visit and admired very much the love you shared; it was magnetic."

"Thank you."

"I am calling to invite you to come here and spend time at my compound in Nueva Gerona. I want you to bring the children and to stay as long as it takes for your heart to heal."

"Thank you, Fidel. I have a church to run. The children are in school."

"You make the calls to your church people and find a replacement. The school is not a problem. They can join Chloe Norma in the school on the compound."

"Chloe?"

"Stanley and Danielle arrived here early this morning along with Doctor Blue on Quinn O'Malley's plane."

"I heard that roar in the middle of the night and wondered!"

"You will love being here with your friends. Your children will enjoy going to school here, learning Spanish, and teaching English. Please do come. Stanley and Danielle are hoping you say yes."

"Why'd they leave in the middle of the night?"

"Quinn O'Malley thought it best."

"Oh. You know what, you're right. I'll talk with our children, and we'll make plans. Thank you, Fidel."

"You are welcome, Katie. Tell them they are invited to Chloe's birthday party next Saturday. She will be sixteen. How do you say it in North America? Sweet sixteen!"

"It will be the glorious adventure we need. Goodbye, Fidel."

Katie stared at the sunset picture on her desk. "Thank you, honey. Fidel Castro just called me. I would have never known this life if I had stayed in Boston. I love you."

CHAPTER 32

THE LIST

Chief of Police Larry Strait's mind instinctively responded to the retort from behind him. The sound of an M21 sniper rifle – the sound protecting him after crash-landing his F-4 Phantom on Ton Duc Thang Boulevard next to the Saigon River – that same sharp crack now came from behind over his right shoulder. The sound echoed off the brick courthouse in front of him right before a second shot. Larry pulled his sidearm and twisted around, looking up at the city center bell tower 200 yards away.

Wyatt Tiffany's big body lurched forward for several shackled steps. A third shot came from the bell tower, exploding the Texan's head before the sound arrived.

Larry emptied his pistol at the open area near the top of the bell tower, below the great clock face. The two state police sergeants assigned to escort prisoner Tiffany to his hearing before Judge Linsenmayer also returned fire at the bell tower until their guns were empty.

Then they turned back and looked at their dead prisoner.

"The vest took the first two," Chief Strait said. "Shit!"

"You guys go; I'll stay here…go!"

The two state policeman ran. Chief Strait radioed for help.

Twenty minutes later they returned. The older of the two held out a three by five-inch piece of white paper with a list written in pencil, scotch tape dangling from the top.

"Found this taped to the bell."

1. Quinn O'Malley
2. Richard Elmore Fortin
3. ~~Wyatt Tiffany~~
4. Doctor A.W. Blue
5. Amy Hamilton
6. Norah Chase
We will win. We always have. This list can grow, if you like.

The Committee

• • •

"Timothy, call Quinn!" Larry Strait ran through Poor Joe's front door.

Timothy looked up from the inventory sheet and tossed his pen on the counter.

"Call Quinn on that yellow phone of yours," he repeated, out of breath, placing the list on the counter. "I need to talk to him."

"What Timothy?" Quinn answered.

"Chief Strait needs to talk with you."

"Quinn, Wyatt Tiffany was just assassinated in front of the courthouse by a sniper hiding in the bell tower. We found a list of names taped on the bell with Tiffany's name crossed out."

"Read me the list."

"You, Richard, A.W, Amy Hamilton, and Norah Chase. A note on the bottom threatens to grow the list. Sent by The Committee."

The phone remained silent for at least ten seconds.

"Larry, get someone over to the school and collect the Chase children; have someone pick up Belvia Chase. Keep them all in your office until I arrive. I'm two hours away, and I'll bring help. Damn those guys. Two hours, Larry."

Quinn pushed the reset button on his Comstat phone which had been on speaker mode. He turned and looked at Amy Hamilton, sitting in a chair next to the sink that smelled of vomit.

"Fair weather friends you've been hanging with, Amy. They're afraid you're going to spill the beans. Gotta hand it to you, you're one tough broad."

"That's a compliment, I guess."

"If only you used your skills for good."

"Tiffany's dead?"

"Sounds like it."

"How do I know this whole thing isn't staged – a phone call on your fancy yellow phone to scare the shit out of me, get me to talk."

"You're free to leave."

"What?"

"Leave. If you think this is a ruse. Leave, and good luck with the committee, whoever the hell they are."

"It's real. I knew when the chief said 'The Committee' it was real."

"You ready to help?"

"Yes."

"Good. Let's go for another helicopter ride."

Quinn untied the rope around her wrists and waist confining her to the wooden chair.

"And just so you know right up front, Miss Hamilton: if you double-cross me, I will personally drop you off on Michigan Avenue in Chicago, wearing a red dress with a target pinned to your back."

Richard walked through the shack's front door, carrying a brown grocery bag.

Quinn shook his head.

"And I was looking forward to those fillets. We've got a problem in Big Bay." Quinn pushed the red button concealed under a protective cap on the Comstat phone.

"We need all hands on deck for an evacuation."

"What about her?" Richard asked, pointing.

"Ask her."

"What?"

"I'll help you guys."

"What changed her mind?"

"Her friends. She's on their hit list."

"Well, ain't that a surprise."

Richard tossed the steaks in the chest freezer.

"Don't be so smug; you're on the list, too," Amy said.

"You know, I'd be disappointed if I wasn't included. Good! Hope they come looking for me," Richard replied. "Where am I on the list, Quinn?"

"Number two. I'm number one. Wyatt Tiffany was number three."

"Was?"

"They shot him today. A sniper hiding in the bell tower shot him on the courthouse steps this morning."

"So, they're not going in order then," Richard quipped.

You have no idea who these people are, Amy thought. She pushed aside a printed cotton window drape and looked through the dirty kitchen window, down the hill at a large lake and a sleek black helicopter, idling on a level spot near the beach.

"Where are we?" she asked.

"Canada," Richard replied.

"Canada is a large place," Amy said with a question in her voice.

"Sure is," Quinn said.

She turned to watch the men packing items in duffle bags.

"You guys learn anything with all those Pentothal doses?" she asked, looking at the reddened intravenous site in her left forearm and rubbing it.

"We learned the names of your first two husbands, that you have slept with Robert Cash but don't like him, and that you love Stanley McMillen — that you wish the cell phone messages you concocted were for real."

CHAPTER 33

JUST IN TIME

Tap…tap…tap…

He pretended to doze in the old cab, his eyes nearly closed, watching the third shift city police crew leaving for the day, walking past his cab in the jail parking lot. He pulled a Chicago Cubs ball cap down further over his forehead. A young policeman tapped on the driver's side window.

The man opened his eyes with a start and rolled the window down partway.

"You can't park here, sir," the tired patrolman said.

"So sorry. Been a long night. I'll move right away."

The Ford Crown Victoria drove slowly around the block then parked on the street within sight of the front door. He stared at the sign in the yard.

CITY OF BIG BAY POLICE DEPARTMENT

Three policemen in their blue uniforms walked around the empty parking lot. Together they stretched yellow barrier tape at all three parking lot entrances – DO NOT CROSS – tying the ends around maple trees. Then each took a position next to an entrance.

The man in the cab watched and listened. Twenty minutes later he tilted his head, watching through the windshield as a sleek helicopter roared over the police department at a high rate of speed. It returned a few minutes later, flying low, before landing in the parking lot. The side door opened, and his pulse quickened slightly, watching Quinn O'Malley and Richard Fortin sprint through the front door. Twenty men dressed in black carrying automatic weapons followed, encircling their flying machine. When he turned his attention back to the helicopter, he thought he recognized Amy Hamilton sitting in a seat against the wall, all alone. The morning sun reflected from something: a sniper rifle. A man kneeling beside the helicopter, peered through the scope, aiming directly at him.

Vladimir started the cab and watched Quinn O'Malley lead Belvia Chase and her three children to the helicopter, followed by Richard Elmore Fortin and Chief Larry Strait.

There will be another time, he thought in Siberian.

Vladimir Khrushchev drove the old cab slowly away, blue smoke trailing behind. He listened to the roar of the jet-powered machine lift behind him and then fly directly above, just low enough so he could see it wag back and forth from side to side, taunting, taunting before it accelerated out of site, in the direction of the Big Bay airport.

...next time, O'Malley...damn...that would have almost completed the list...

● ● ●

Katherine Kennedy McGinnis sat for several minutes, staring at the gleeful sunset picture of her and Doug before quietly walking to the living room. She stood and watched her children on the couch and big armchair, facing the television, absorbed in the Disney channel. She looked at young Doug, now eleven. They had adopted him eleven years ago when he was one month old, after his mother Sarah had died, and somehow Richard Elmore Fortin had convinced Sarah's parents to drop their protest. Now he sat in Doug's big chair. On the couch sat the three children they'd adopted following their mother's murder by her estranged husband. Beth looked more and more like her mother, Tiffany, and at age fourteen, she seemed more withdrawn, especially now. Joey looked older than thirteen. He and

Doug competed now to be the man in the family. Seven-year-old Jamie looked the most like her mom and seemed the happiest.

Katie reached for the remote and muted the sound.

"MOM!" they exclaimed in unison.

She pulled over the old milking bench that Doug had used for a footrest and sat in front of the television.

"Chloe's having a birthday party next Saturday. We're all invited."

"Let's go to Target and buy presents!" Jamie exclaimed.

"Why didn't she mention something to me?" Beth muttered.

"Well, Beth, I bet she would have if she had known. It's a surprise party."

"Her mom?" Beth retorted.

"Nope. This is a very special party being thrown by the president of Cuba."

Her four children stared at her.

"Fidel Castro is coming back here?" Joey asked, vaguely recalling the great celebration at Poor Joe's.

"Nope, we get to go to Cuba."

Beth smiled, which thrilled Katie. "We're studying the Caribbean in world history. I would love to tell everybody I went to Cuba."

Katie stood and resumed the sound. She walked back to her office, listening to her children excitedly discuss all the things they would do in Cuba.

"I'm going to taste that rum," Beth said, and little Jamie said, "Me, too!"

Doug and Joey agreed they would sneak some Cuban cigars home with them.

● ● ●

Fidel Castro fumbled and dropped his phone after retrieving it from his shirt pocket.

"Fidel, it's Katie. We want to come."

"I just spoke with Quinn. He is sending his plane to Big Bay today. I will have him call you. Is that too soon?"

"No, it's not too soon; it's just in time."

"He will call you soon."

Katie walked back to the living room. "TV off. Everyone go pack an overnight bag; we are going to Cuba today!"

"MOM! REALLY?"

"Really."

Katie's cell phone rang.

"Quinn here, Katie. My plane just left London. It should arrive there in three hours. You and the kids pack light. I'll have two guys pick you up. They'll be driving a black Hummer."

"OK."

"Katie, there is a situation unfolding as we speak. Belvia and her kids will be at the airport to travel to Cuba with you. If anyone other than two men dressed in black driving a Hummer show up, lock the doors and call the police. I don't expect any trouble; just a precaution."

"Thanks for the heads up. Quinn. Doug would be loading his shotgun about now."

"That he would, Katie. That he would. See you soon in Cuba. I hear we have a birthday party next Saturday."

●●●

At the airport, in the private hangar next to the main terminal, seven children scurried about, ecstatic to discover they were all going to the birthday party in Cuba together.

"Chloe will be so surprised to see us!" seven-year-old Jamie exclaimed, scampering up the steps. "Mom, we need to get her a present from Cuba!"

The True Believers, surrounding their idling helicopter and airplane, laughed.

"What were all those men with guns doing here?" Joey asked.

"This is a very important plane," young Doug replied with authority. "Probably there are people who would steal it."

● ● ●

Vladimir Khrushchev watched the children and their mothers get on the supersonic plane. He peered through powerful binoculars from the woods on the west side of Airport Road, hidden under the big trees at the end of the runway. He watched the helicopter rise straight up, nearly out of sight while the sleek jet taxied to the far end of the runway and turned around.

*Time's up…checkmate…*He twisted his Chicago Cubs ball cap backward.

The speck in the distance accelerated quickly toward him before the loud roar arrived.

Vladimir flipped the safety off and hoisted the surface-to-air missile launcher to his right shoulder. He turned, waiting for the plane to fly overhead. Looking up, his baseball cap fell.

…wait…wait…wait…die!…

Gently, he pulled on the trigger, harder and then harder. The heat-seeking missile launched from the tube through an opening in the treetops, locking on the heat roaring from the rear of the jet.

Alarms sounded in the cockpit. The pilot and copilot surveyed the blinking red lights and radar screen.

"Oh shit!" the pilot exclaimed.

The autopilot took control of the Gulfstream. The plane veered sharply to the right, flying in a tight circle while accelerating.

Loose stuff inside the passenger compartment rose and floated for an instant before slamming to the port wall and sticking as if glued.

Seven-year-old Jamie lifted with the debris and joined the stuff glued to the wall above the seats, looking down, laughing.

"This is fun!" she screamed.

Through their windows on the left side of the plane, the pilots and passengers saw a bright explosion about 100 yards away.

The concussion forced the tail down, spinning the plane like an old windmill. The autopilot engaged emergency thrusters; the nose rotated up from pointing down, launching the jet straight up and out of sight.

Little Jamie flew past and landed against the rear wall. From against the restroom door she gazed up at everyone twisting around in their seats, looking back in terror. The plane continued to accelerate straight up. When it reached 65,000 feet, it leveled off and headed south; traveling at 1,500 miles per hour.

"Look Mom…bloody nose!" Jamie exclaimed, standing up, rubbing under her pixie nose. "I never had a bloody nose before!"

"The bogies work, can't wait to tell Quinn, the bogies work!" the pilot said, high-fiving the copilot.

"This is more fun than the fair rides," young Doug exclaimed.

The pale mothers glanced at each other.

"Jamie, you sit right here and keep the seat belt buckled," Katie said sternly while concealing a smile of relief, wiping away the blood from her daughter's first nose bleed.

Vladimir threw the missile launcher to the ground in disgust.

…where does Quinn get these toys…

He picked up the launcher off the ground and headed for the Crown Victoria's open trunk, looking up just in time to see a Gatling gun emerge from the underbelly of the rapidly approaching black helicopter.

Vladimir took three running steps.

In an instant, the old cab became smoldering scrap metal with a former life form next to it. The flying machine hovered above, seemingly in anger, repeatedly sending torrents of lead into the mangled mess, and making mush of the once-human form, now unidentifiable, splattering tiny bone fragments on the tree trunks. Only a Cubs hat remained intact.

"There, Quinn," Richard said through the intercom from the navigator's seat. "That's one off our list."

Amy listened in her headset, sitting beside Quinn, in a compartment packed with True Believers.

"Hey Grandpa, can I fly her for just a little bit? Please?"

"Sure, just don't let him try to land it, Mark."

Amy looked at Quinn, feeling the machine accelerate to 400 miles per hour.

Quinn leaned close to Amy.

"Before he lost his right eye, Richard was the best helicopter pilot in the United States Air Force."

"Oh."

"No depth perception now; can't land worth a damn."

"Oh."

"He'd do it, too, and likely we'd be OK. The situation is this: Richard has no fear of death, while these guys would just as soon have a few more nights with their ladies." He nodded at the True Believers.

"That's what's different about him. I wondered. Why, is he crazy?"

"Nope. Ask him sometime about Nicaragua, about Honduras, about his little sister Marie."

Amy looked closely at Quinn's face.

Quinn shrugged.

"He's died before, Amy. He says it's kinda fun. Says you can hear the colors."

"We'll refuel in Key West and head to Nueva Gerona, general," the pilot said over the intercom.

"Nueva Gerona?" Amy asked.

"Cuba," Quinn replied. "We have a birthday party to attend."

"And," he continued, "you have some apologizing to do."

Amy watched Quinn push a sequence of numbers and letters on his Comstat phone.

"On my way to Nueva Gerona…They need you in Big Bay, Victor."

When he put the Comstat phone in his pocket, Amy asked, "Whose birthday?"

"Chloe Norma McMillen. She's turning sixteen this Saturday."

Amy Hamilton stared at the floor. She folded her fingers together.

…damn…

"Hey, Richard just called you Grandpa."

"His warped sense of humor."

"He said Grandpa bailed him out of that Tennessee jail."

"Yeah, I guess he did."

CHAPTER 34

RC WITH A SHOT

It felt morose for a poker night, thick, gray and weighty.

Doug's chair in the middle of the long table leaned forward, the back resting on the table edge with a green bar towel draped on the back. Katie's chair and Stanley's too, both empty. In the booth next to the popcorn machine, usually occupied by teenagers with raging pheromones, sat Charles Dwight Fife, all alone, reading a *Mad Magazine*.

The booth where the ladies always sat, under the stuffed badger clinging to the wall, had no occupants.

Doctor McCaferty held high the morning edition of the *Big Bay Recorder*, and read the headlines out loud.

"'State Police request FBI assistance.' 'Chief Strait calls Airport Road explosions mysterious.' Sub-headline: 'Investigation on Administrator Tiffany's murder ongoing.'"

"Mysterious, Larry?" a frowning Pete asked.

"Sure is. We found a serial number on what's left of a rear axle, 1985 Ford Crown Victoria, last registered to a Chicago taxi company which went out of business nine years ago."

"All that racket and explosion when Quinn's plane took off. Attributed to sonic boom, says here in the paper," Jack commented.

"Seemed a little early for a sonic boom," Wayne added.

Chief of Police Larry Strait smiled. "Yup, I thought so, too. That's why I turned the investigation over to the state police, and now they've called the FBI. All quite mysterious."

The brand new wooden screen door, still unpainted, squeaked and slammed shut. Victor Bonifacio walked in.

"I need a drink."

"RC?" Timothy inquired, reaching for Victor's favorite beverage.

"With a shot of Jack Daniels."

"Victor, you don't drink," Machete proclaimed from the table end, thinking back over the many years he had known the Minneapolis Godfather and True Believer.

"I gave that up as a bad habit. Make it a double shot, Timothy."

Victor looked all around the old bar and at each booth before he sat down in Katie's designated poker night chair, across from Doug's tilted chair.

"Quinn advised me of the situation here," Victor said, staring at the newspaper sprawled in front of Doctor McCaferty. "Quinn's worried, a little."

Timothy handed Victor a tall glass filled with ice cubes and RC Cola.

"Just one shot, Victor, training wheels still on, buddy."

"I suspect the people who lived through the horrors of past wars felt the world coming to an end. There are days I have those feelings. Even in my line of work, the olive oil import business, things have changed. There were rules, understandings not to be violated or there would be consequences. Just behave, work hard, and show respect; business went fine and we looked out for each other. Citizens received their products and we made a living. Even our friend Rose, in her line of work, is dismayed. Rose runs a respectable, compassionate business. She has always personally interviewed each of her ladies before hiring them. She looked for honesty and strong character. She's hired nurses and other college graduates over the years, even a lawyer once by the name of Vicki. When she discovered problems with drugs, she intervened and got them help. She's helped them through personal crises and health problems. I have never met one lady who did not love Rose."

Victor took a long drink from the tall glass. He smiled at Timothy and nodded for more.

Young Charles Fife listened from the popcorn booth and glanced at his dad, bringing Victor another tall glass with a single shot.

"Things are changing quickly. The days when we were dealing with simple cartels like the Veracruz bunch in Mexico are gone. *The Company* controls the drug distribution worldwide. It's ruthless and driven by greed, but more than greed, it is driven by the lust for power. *The Company* runs the world by proxy. They have governments in their grasp all over the world, even here in the United States. It's a perverse time, when young girls are sold like goats and drugs like soft drinks to keep people dependent and beholding."

"Well, shit," Wayne uttered. "Any hope at all?"

"Yes." Victor replied, after he finished the second glass. "I think so. If the good people living in this world do not roll over and play dead. I think so."

He reached over and pulled the *Big Bay Recorder* to him.

"You know the FBI will be looking for Quinn after this, right Larry?"

"Yup."

"They have three pieces of the puzzle. On radar they saw a surface-to-air missile being fired in the direction of Quinn's jet leaving Big Bay. They saw the jet go through evasive measures and send out numerous bogies to confuse the rocket. And then they saw the rocket explode a safe distance away. They know that civilian jets don't have those capabilities. They have the missile launcher found in the woods next to the Crown Victoria, which, by the way, is almost unidentifiable as an automobile. They still have no idea who the puddle of protein is next to a Chicago Cubs baseball cap."

Chief Strait smiled. "I bet they never saw Quinn's helicopter."

"That part has them confused. But they know he and Castro have them, so that's the FBI's working hypothesis."

Victor took a small sip.

"All that being said, right now Quinn is worried about you guys. I've reserved twenty rooms at the hotel. If we can find another twenty rooms in town, I'll arrange for a business convention of the Italian Olive Oil Importers, and we'll keep an eye on things for a bit."

"Thanks, Victor, thanks. You want another Jack and RC?"

"Yes, then a ride to the hotel, please."

CHAPTER 35

A YELLOW 1973 SUPER BEETLE

A pink twilight had been nearly absorbed by the darkness when the landing pad lights at the bottom of the sloping lawn flashed on.

The children looked away from their dominos table toward the light. Stanley took another puff on his Hemingway Reserve cigar before placing it in the alabaster ash tray. Belvia and Danielle joined them on the outdoor patio, looking in the direction of the distant *chop-chop-chopping* sounds and ever nearing whine of jet turbines. Chloe ran from her bedroom.

They watched the German-designed stealth helicopter swoop down into the light and softly land.

"And you doubted me," Richard said through the intercom headphones.

"Damn you, Mark," Quinn replied.

Stanley, Danielle, and Chloe started walking down the lighted pathway toward the landing pad. The helicopter side door flopped down when they were about twenty feet away.

Richard exited first, still grinning from his soft landing and Quinn's reaction.

Quinn walked down the ramp, followed by Amy Hamilton.

Stanley stopped and stared.

"What the hell!"

"What, Daddy?"

Stanley reached for his daughter's arm but missed.

"That's Amy Hamilton," her mother said.

Chloe looked at Danielle for a very few seconds before she turned and walked rapidly toward Richard, Quinn, and Amy.

"It's the birthday girl!" Quinn said with a big smile on his weathered face, his arms outstretched.

Richard's head turned, watching Chloe practically run past him.

Chloe ignored Quinn's arms.

"YOU ARE AMY HAMILTON!"

Amy took several steps backward, away from the teenager, before answering, "Yes, I am."

"STAY AWAY FROM MY DAD!"

Chloe turned and shouted at Quinn, "WHAT THE HELL, UNCLE QUINN!" before turning back and facing Amy. They were the same height, which pleased Chloe.

"Get back in there," Chloe said, pointing at the open door. "Right now, get back in there. We're going to talk."

Chloe followed Amy back up the ramp.

"You guys leave," Chloe said to the amused True Believers.

Stanley and Danielle stood still next to Quinn and Richard.

"She's not armed, is she?" Quinn said with a grin.

"Holy shit, I wouldn't want to be the guy that crosses her," Richard said. "She get that from you, Danielle?"

They listened.

"You tried to hurt my dad."

"Yes, I did."

"And then you tried to hurt my mom."

"Yes."

"And you hurt me. You sent me that phone with lies on it."

"Yes, I did that. I'm sorry."

"Why?"

"It's just business, Chloe. You wouldn't understand."

"Probably not. Explain it to me."

Stanley and Danielle looked at each other.

"Jeez, honey, did you know she could be like this?"

"A lot like her daddy," Danielle replied.

Katie, Dora, and Belvia walked down the hill and joined the group.

"I was under a lot of pressure from the home office to get a contract with the Big Bay Hospital and your dad wasn't going for it, so I tried to blackmail him. I really needed to get that contract, and I thought his vote was crucial."

"So you hurt my dad over money?"

"It was more than that. I had a quota. A lot of pressure."

"Like I said, you hurt my dad and mom because of money."

Amy started to stand. "I think we're done here, Chloe. SCREW THIS! I don't have to explain myself to a teenager."

"SIT DOWN, UNCLE QUINN!"

Amy looked out to see Quinn motioning for her to sit down.

"So you think you can hurt me and my parents and then just show up here and ruin my birthday party, too?"

"I won't be at your party."

Amy took a deep breath and looked at Chloe.

"I did what I did because I feared for my life. I worked for some dangerous people."

"And you made a lot of money."

"I did."

"Worth it? Going around hurting people, just to make a lot of money, worried you might get blotted out or something? Worth it?"

"It's a slippery slope."

"Right, whatever that means. I hope you're happy now. What are you doing here?"

Amy looked at the floor for a few seconds.

"I'm here to apologize to you, to your mother, and your father. I'm sorry, Chloe."

"You really? Or you just saying that cuz Uncle Quinn made you?"

"Well, you have me there. I admit your Uncle Quinn and Richard have a way of persuading. But, I'm serious. I am sorry."

"Why, because you're busted?"

"Because," Amy said, "because I was wrong, and now I have an opportunity to make it right. That is why, Chloe; that, and the fact that when I was your age, I was in love with your father. I thought we were in love with each other."

Danielle tilted her head sideways and stared at her husband.

Stanley grimaced.

●●●

Friday morning President Castro flew from his residence in Havana to Nueva Gerona. The ground crew pushed his helicopter aside on the tarmac, and a second helicopter arrived. Marco and Marciana Gonzales had arrived, too, on the very spot Stanley had married them.

Debra joined Katie, Dora, Danielle, Marciana, and Belvia, climbing into Castro's limousine. A smiling lieutenant drove slowly down the great hill overlooking the ocean, taking the ladies downtown, shopping for the sixteenth birthday bash.

"Quinn and I have a little something needs done," Fidel said to Stanley and Marco. He grasped Quinn's arm and they walked toward a military Jeep.

"You drive, Quinn. My eyes are getting foggy."

From the brick patio, Stanley and Doctor Gonzales watched the two old friends drive down the hill in a green military Jeep with a Cuban flag flapping from a slender pole attached to the rear bumper.

"There go a couple of true visionaries," said a shaky old voice.

Stanley and Marco turned. Behind them stood Doctor A.W. Blue, wearing a blue suit.

Doctor Gonzales stared silently at the thin old man.

Stanley said to Marco, "Marco, I want you to meet a legend. This is your predecessor, Fidel's physician before you, Doctor A.W. Blue."

A.W. smiled while extending his skinny hand.

"Doctor Blue…I thought you were dead. Fidel told me you were lost at sea."

"In a way, that is true."

The doctors shook hands and then Marco pulled A.W. closer and put his arm on his shoulder.

"I have heard much about you," the young doctor said in Spanish.

"Fidel tells me you are a superior physician, that you saved his life," A.W. replied in Spanish.

"Stanley and Danielle helped."

"Come on, guys, no Spanish," Stanley complained. "Lina, would you bring us some coffee?"

"You want to hear a wild story?" A.W. asked, sitting in a white wicker chair.

"Yes, I would," Marco replied. He sat next to the old doctor.

"You ever been to St. Kitts?"

"Have not."

"I have…."

"May I join you?" Amy Hamilton poked her head through the open sliding glass doors.

A.W. Blue looked at Amy, standing next to Stanley's chair, for several seconds before he answered, "Yes, please do. I think you need to hear this story."

●●●

"Can you believe Amy Hamilton and Stan dated in high school and he never told me?" Danielle said, walking along on the sidewalk next to 35th Street.

"Sure," Debra said, "he loves you."

"What does that mean?"

"He's just protecting you. Stanley adores you. Have you told him about your high school loves?"

…Jimmy Glenn…Joel Lagasse…

"No."

"That's what I mean. What's the point? The future is in front, Danielle. You guys are always planning exciting things; to hell with the past. I know, trust me." Debra flashed a smile.

"You're right. Just shocked, I guess?"

"You must admit, she has a good taste in men," Marciana interjected in her thick Cuban accent.

"Oh, shut up." Danielle laughed.

"Let's have lunch here," Dora pointed at the sign, PIZZERIA LA GONDOLA.

"Fidel and I love this pizza."

"And we can order mojitos," Katie said. "We have a driver."

●●●

"Take the roundabout and the north exit to the Servi-Cupet gas station," Fidel said in Spanish.

"Gas gauge is on full."

"Birthday present; you'll see."

Three gas station attendants stood stiff, almost at attention, watching the presidential Jeep drive over the pneumatic hose, causing the bell to ring twice, coming to a stop next to a shiny yellow Volkswagen Beetle.

"She's a beauty," Fidel said. "They've checked it out and fixed everything – new brakes, rebuilt engine, wiper motor, everything!" He smiled a big smile.

"A 1973 Super Beetle. I had one in Berlin!" Quinn said.

"Think Chloe will like it?"

"She'll be thrilled. Can she drive?" Quinn looked inside. "She'll have to shift a manual."

"How hard can it be? You got us here."

The chief attendant approached, hesitantly, holding the keys.

"We'll put these in a nice little box. Please have this delivered tomorrow at two; bring it on your big truck. I will leave instructions for the guards to let you through," Fidel said to the young man.

"Stanley and Danielle know what you're up to?" Quinn asked, walking back to the Jeep.

"They do not!" Fidel laughed. "Drive over to 26th Street."

"Why?"

"Restaurante El Dragon. You will like it."

● ● ●

They watched the green Jeep driving up the hill from the patio, its Cuban flag flapping in the warm wind.

Stanley could not tell who looked paler, Marco or Amy, after A.W. finished reciting the past ten years.

Amy twisted in her chair, watching the girls play dominos and practice Spanish words on each other. She watched Norah Chase laughing, wearing the worn New York Yankees baseball cap that she treasured.

...that poor girl...

● ● ●

Chloe's birthday party started at twelve noon on Saturday.

Children from the island grade school and Chloe's tenth grade classes all came. Children ran here and there, playing games on the lawn organized by Lina and several presidential guards.

The lunch, consisting of hamburgers, hot dogs, potato chips, and barbecued chicken with black beans and rice, thrilled the children. "*Tanto... Tanto...*(so much)... *Tan bueno!...*(so good)..." was repeated over and over as the kids, at first hesitantly and then with enthusiasm, returned to the serving tables for seconds and thirds.

"We should make sure they take all the leftovers home," Katie said to Dora, watching the children's wide eyes. Dora whispered in Fidel's ear. He nodded yes.

Chloe blew out sixteen candles mounted on a giant white cake, Lina's pride, at 2:00 p.m. A big flatbed truck groaned up the steep hill. Secured on the truck's wooden bed rested a yellow VW Beetle with a giant ribbon through the front windows tied in a red bow on the top.

"Daddy!" Chloe screamed, jumping up and down.

Stanley looked at Danielle who shook her head no.

Fidel winked at the McMillens.

Stanley glanced at Quinn, who quickly looked in the opposite direction, hiding his smile.

The adults watched Chloe and Norah climb into the front seats and then Norah climbed out, tilting the passenger seat forward, filling the rear seat with Beth and giggling youngsters until only heads poked over the front seats.

"She doesn't have a driver's license, Fidel," Stanley said.

"There's one in the glove box with a presidential seal," Fidel said, grinning a big grin, leaning on his cane. "She's so excited!"

He looked at Chloe's parents. "I love that child."

CHAPTER 36

A PROBLEM IN NICARAGUA

Robert Cash studied the faces all around the table. His steely, cold, blue eyes stopped on Ivan.

"Any news from Vladimir on the Big Bay project?"

Ivan squirmed in his chair.

"The good news…Vladimir dispatched Tiffany with his sniper rifle."

"Good. What else?"

"Vladimir is dead."

Silence.

Angry silence stifled the room.

"How?" Robert asked.

"He'd just fired a heat seeker at O'Malley's jet. They ambushed him from behind. Shot him from a helicopter with a Gatling gun. Our informant told me the car looked like confetti and so did Vladimir."

"Did he hit the plane?"

"No. Our informant says the plane sent out bogies and took evasive action."

Robert Cash rubbed both eyes and leaned back in his chair.

…shit…what the hell…

"Rum!" he commanded.

John Hall cleared his throat.

"What John?"

"The bio-research lab in Nicaragua reports a problem."

"Please do share," Robert said sarcastically.

"The hybrid Asian Tiger Mosquito lives less than twenty-four hours after being infected with the mutated H1N3 virus. After the South African experiments, they now realize the virus will not spread from person to person. The only way to be infected is by the female mosquito bite. Our guys spread the virus on door handles and such – nothing – only the mosquito bite. And these hybrids only feed when it's above seventy-five Fahrenheit. So we have a very short period of time to transport infected mosquitoes from Matagalpa to wherever and hope that it's warm."

"How about satellite labs?"

"The bio-guys say no; they are struggling to keep the one lab up and running."

Robert took a particularly long drink from his rum tumbler.

"Anybody else with some good news?"

He took another gulp of rum, crunching the ice with his teeth.

"OK, then, we've lost our number one and most effective enforcer. We've got others. So our mosquito virus thing is not maturing as rapidly as we had hoped. Give those smart guys in Nicaragua a chance; they'll figure it out."

He paused, scratching his beard.

"Here's some good news."

He handed his empty rum tumbler to a guard for a refill.

"Everyone on the list is in Cuba at Castro's retreat."

He reached for the refreshed tumbler.

"No one outside of this room needs to know about this mosquito problem. Just the fear of the possibility will suffice. Our immediate problem is dealing with angry clients. I have several princes demanding their down payments returned. We need a new clinic opened soon."

Chewing ice, he continued, "Amy Hamilton is with them in Cuba."

He took another gulp.

"And, she has their trust."

CHAPTER 37

THE MENU

Moses' blue eyes twinkled.

She handed a shiny menu to Timothy and a cup of black coffee. "Jenifer Gomez at The Havana Cafe helped me."

Stanley sipped the coffee and looked at chuckling Machete. "You in on this, Machete?"

"It's a beauty!" Machete replied, looking at the new menu with his blind eyes.

Poor Joe's Menu
Cinnamon Nut Roll $2.00
Croissant (your choice)....................$2.50
Eggs Benedict.................................$9.50
Omelet (your choice)....................$10.00
Crepes (Chef's choice) $7.50
Hot Beef Baguettes........................$10.50
Grilled Ham/Cheese........................$6.50
Dora's Famous Clam Chowder.........$6.00
Timothy's Chili $6.00
Pepperoni Pizza $15.00
Dessert Crepes.................................$8.00
Popcorn... Free
Beer................................. Free Tomorrow

"How'd you get these printed," Timothy asked, "without consulting with the owner? That's me, Moses."

"You like it? I added de pizza for all de olive oil guys hanging around. De free beer at de bottom be Machete's idea. Ain't it fine?"

"How much?"

"Nothing. Jenifer had them made for my welcome gift."

Timothy took a deep breath.

"You put her in charge," Machete said. "I heard you. You said, 'You're in charge of the kitchen; let me know if you have questions.' She didn't."

Timothy rubbed at his eyes and looked at beaming Moses then at grinning Machete.

"I'm not sure I can afford to have you two in cahoots."

"Here, try dis pear almond croissant." Moses handed Timothy a warm roll. Her smiled warmed Timothy all over.

"Hey, Timothy, did ya see the new menu?" Wayne inquired, walking down the stairs.

Timothy shook his head.

"I like de olive oil guys," Moses said. "Dey tip great. And did you see dey have guns under deir jackets?"

"You don't miss a thing, do you?" Timothy said, now smiling.

"No sir. A girl named Moses don't miss much, mister."

Moses carried a plate with two warm apple croissants to Machete. She sat next to the blind little Mexican and stroked Little Miss several times. Then the two grasped hands and bowed their heads for a few seconds.

"We both have much we be thankful for," Moses said, when she noticed Timothy and Wayne staring.

●●●

"You were in on it; you teach her how to drive a stick shift, Uncle Quinn," Stanley said, watching his daughter along with Beth and Norah sitting in her birthday present, chattering.

"Fidel's idea," Quinn replied, nudging the president of Cuba. Richard grinned.

Marco and A.W. joined the men drinking coffee on the red brick patio.

Lina put a fresh pitcher of dark coffee on their table.

"She gonna kill herself in that car," Lina commented, shaking her head.

Fidel grinned.

"Look at her; look at those young ladies. This might be the happiest years of their lives," the president of Cuba said. For a second, his expression looked sad.

"OK, I'll do it; where are the keys?"

Fidel reached into his shirt pocket and handed them to Quinn.

"The safety brake works; I made sure they tested it," Fidel shouted at his old friend walking the slope toward the giggling girls.

The men on the patio watched Norah join Beth in the back seat while Quinn took the passenger seat next to an excited Chloe.

The little air cooled engine started.

Quinn explained the clutching and shifting to Chloe one more time.

The yellow car lurched forward and stalled.

The men on the patio listened to the hysterical laughter coming from the VW. Quinn laughed the loudest.

"Start it again, honey."

CHAPTER 38

MEN CAN'T HELP THEMSELVES

Over the years, the formal dining room located on the top floor of Castro's three story villa had been used for international negotiations and private affairs of state.

It is a large round room sixty feet in diameter with walls consisting of brass-framed, thick glass windows extending from the floor to the ceiling overlooking the ocean. It has a domed ceiling constructed of mahogany. A large grand piano sits next to an oak desk. The round oak dining table fills the middle of the room, large enough to seat thirty people.

Victor Bonifacio had flown in from Minneapolis on Quinn's jet Monday morning. After a conversation with Rose in Las Vegas, Quinn sent his plane back to pick her up and then to Big Bay to pick up Timothy.

The True Believers sat around the large table Tuesday morning. Fidel Castro and Quinn O'Malley sat side by side, as always, looking at Victor, Stanley, Marco, Richard, Rose, Timothy, Dora, and A.W. Blue. Amy Hamilton sat at the table too, across from Stanley.

"Thanks everyone for coming," Quinn said. "And welcome to our newest member. After all he has experienced and witnessed, Fidel and I thought it entirely appropriate for A.W. to join us."

Rose started to clap and then everyone clapped.

"Amy contacted Robert Cash. He seemed somewhat eager to have a discussion," Victor said, nodding in her direction.

"Mister Cash indicated an interest in meeting. He's concerned for his safety given the St. Kitts events," Amy said, her eyes moving from one True Believer to the next while she spoke.

Rose stared at Amy, watching her eyes and hands.

"What'd you think of that St. Kitts operation?" Rose asked Amy.

"I just learned about it from Doctor Blue. It sounds abhorrent," Amy replied.

Rose and Amy locked eyes.

"You've slept with him, haven't you?"

"Why would you think that?"

The men around the table watched the women lock horns.

"The way you held your hands, the way you curled your finger when you said his name. You called him mister. I've interviewed hundreds of young ladies; you've had sex with that man."

Amy's eyes flashed at Stanley for an instant before locking on Rose again.

"Well?"

"He told you," Amy retorted, pointing at Richard.

"Now, Amy, do I look like that kinda guy? Quinn and I haven't said a word. Did you tell anyone, Quinn?"

Quinn shook his head *no*.

"Well?"

Amy glared at Rose.

"It really is of no concern of mine, who you choose to have sex with, Amy, or why. I'm just making a point. Don't try to pull a fast one. I can read you like a book. And, Amy, I'm a speed reader. You understand?"

"Yes."

"Good. We can proceed, Quinn."

Quinn smiled. "And don't forget about the red dress and Michigan Avenue."

Richard smiled.

Fidel looked puzzled.

"Amy, we want you to call Robert Cash again. Tell him this

committee would like to meet with his committee. We'll agree to meet at a neutral location to be chosen no longer than twenty-four hours before the meeting. Anywhere will be just fine. Both committees, face-to-face, anyplace in the world. Call him."

Quinn slid an inexpensive cell phone across the smooth tabletop to her.

"Call him."

Amy opened the flip phone and punched in a series of numbers. Rose watched and smiled

...knows his number by heart...

"Robert, it's Amy."

"Where are you?"

"Nowhere special."

"You're not alone, are you?"

"No, not really. I talked with O'Malley, like you asked."

"He's in the room with you, isn't he?

"Yes."

"Dammit, Amy, hand him the phone."

"Hello, Robert Cash. Looking forward to our little meeting."

"I as well, Quinn O'Malley. You're a boil on my butt; just keeps festering and causing me agony."

Quinn laughed and looked at Amy with a nod.

"Yes, she can be, Robert, true enough. Now listen, we saw Vladimir's hit list, hand-written in pencil, before we sent him to explain himself to The Almighty. I'm not going to share our list, other than to tell you Vladimir was number two. Now, we'll honor a truce, if you agree, and we'll meet."

"I'll discuss it with my committee and get back with you at this number," Robert retorted.

"This is Amy's phone; you'll have to call her. Here she is; tell her you still love her, Robert."

Quinn slid the open phone back to Amy.

"Hello...?"

"He's gone."

"Thanks, Amy. You can leave now. Let us know what he comes up with. Take that phone with you," Quinn said.

● ● ●

Amy pushed the elevator button. The door opened and a young man, *about thirty,* Amy thought, wearing a green military uniform, stepped out as she entered.

"You will remember, I am sure, my chief of staff, General Juan Castro," Fidel said.

Rose frowned.

"He led a breakaway battalion in Cardenas to protect the president during an assassination attempt; promoted from corporal to general in one week," Stanley said, leaning to his left and touching Rose.

"Oh, I remember him. He traveled with President Castro to Big Bay for Marco's wedding reception."

"That's him."

The chief of staff handed Fidel a note.

"Well, what do you know," Fidel said, "technology is astounding. Mister Robert Cash is in Nicaragua."

"Did we get the exact coordinates?" Richard asked.

Fidel handed the paper back to Juan.

"Latitude 12.9167 north, Longitude 85.9167 west. The exact location is Cathedral San Pedro."

"In a church; ain't that about right," Timothy muttered.

"Doesn't seem right, blowing a church to smithereens," Stanley said.

"He knows that's the way we think; that's no accident, Stan," Quinn said.

"Where's their lab?" Rose asked.

"One moment, I will return," Juan Castro said.

"What we can do is blow that lab at the same instant we have team Mongoose hit the cathedral. Get Amy Hamilton back here," Rose demanded.

Quinn smiled and shook his head. Fidel smiled, too.

Five minutes later, Amy walked off the elevator.

"You don't need to sit down. Just answer this: is the lab that Oleson Pharmaceuticals owns in Matagalpa the only place they have the virus?"

"Where?"

"Lina, bring that red dress out here!" Quinn yelled through cupped hands at the serving area.

Lina walked out holding a crimson red dress on a hanger, un-zipped in the back.

"Yup, that'll look great on Michigan Avenue. Thanks, Lina."

Juan Castro returned.

"The laboratory in question is located six blocks directly west of the San Pedro Cathedral."

"Oh, you mean in Nicaragua!" Amy stared at the red dress.

"You know exactly what we mean. You don't sleep with a man as many times as you slept with Robert Cash without learning most everything. A little booze, a lot of sex, men can't help themselves, blabbing, trying to impress their ladies with power. Told you not to mess with me, Amy."

For the first time, Rose watched fear form in Amy's eyes.

"I'm dead if I talk."

"We're all dead eventually; question is how soon. You want to talk or take a trip north to Chicago with Quinn?"

"Amy," Richard said, "you know your name is on *The Company's* list. Help us here, and we'll make sure you disappear safely."

"They have been trying to reproduce the hybrid tiger mosquito infected with the mutated virus at other labs. Hasn't worked. They've got problems keeping them alive in Matagalpa; live less than a day."

"So, this is the only place in the world where this virus exists?" Quinn asked.

"As far as I know, yes."

"Good. You can go now. I'll take your phone."

She handed Quinn the flip phone.

"The other one, too."

Amy opened her purse and handed Quinn her smart phone.

Amy stepped in the elevator. She stared at Stanley through the closing doors.

"We go tonight," Quinn said toward Richard. "Team Mongoose and your flying wing, Fidel. We go tonight."

Richard smiled.

"I love that machine."

CHAPTER 39

THE GHOST WING

He had flown in the flying wing, nicknamed the *Ghost Wing,* powered by neutron thrusters, only once before – on a mission to obliterate the Veracruz compound in Mexico City, late one night on day two of a cartel summit meeting. Mexico City's newspaper, *Aristegui Noticias,* ran this headline the following morning:

"*METEORITO DESTRUYE COMPUESTO RADIACTIVO FAMILIA VERACRUZ*"

Richard smiled, riding in the Jeep toward the military airport outside of Havana.

Team Mongoose had already taken flight in their stealth helicopter. Thirty minutes from their target, the helicopter sent a signal for the flying wing to launch.

It made almost no noise, speeding down the San Antonio de los Baños Airfield runway, only a whoosh lifting off. When it reached the altitude of 60,000 feet, the *Ghost Wing* accelerated to Mach 4 in the direction of Matagalpa, Nicaragua.

Richard sat in the navigator's seat, adjusting dials and watching an infrared screen showing the earth traveling rapidly below.

• • •

Traveling at 400 miles per hour, the XS-1 stealth helicopter carrying Team Mongoose traveled from Cuba to Nicaragua in just under two hours. The Flying Wing with Richard Elmore Fortin in the navigator's seat flew the same distance in twelve minutes. When the stealth airplane reached the Nicaraguan coastline, it slowed to 400 miles per hour and soon began circling Matagalpa, waiting for the signal from Quinn.

Twenty True Believers landed on Highway 3, where the Rio Grande Matagalpa River bends close. Dressed in black, they ran into the darkness, following the river for six blocks then two blocks toward the cathedral.

"GPS coordinated and locked," Richard said from the navigator's seat. "Computer adjustments made for wind shear. I'm ready."

Team Mongoose invaded the large, white, masonry, two-story cathedral through every door simultaneously, at midnight. Quietly – like a cougar stalking…quietly…quietly – from room to room, through the dark sanctuary illuminated faintly by flickering prayer candles at the feet of Jesus, they moved up the stairs to various second story rooms and then to the two towers on either side of the entrance.

On the wide window ledge below the glassless window in the bell tower, a cell phone rang. A True Believer moved close to the phone and, for an instant, illuminated the phone with a pencil flashlight. He broke radio silence.

"Cell phone ringing in the bell tower," he radioed to Quinn in the helicopter hovering above the cathedral.

"Let them leave a message. *Ghost Wing,* fire at will."

Richard lifted the protective cap covering a small red button and pushed it, sending a GPS guided uranium-nitrogen-magnesium incendiary rocket into the center of the pharmaceutical lab. The building imploded, the walls collapsing into a brilliantly burning hole deep into the earth.

"Mission accomplished. Number three off the list. That'll cook those viruses," Richard radioed to Quinn.

"Team Mongoose return to rendezvous point. See everyone at home for debriefing."

●●●

Chloe had wept most of the night. From her second story bedroom she watched the eastern sky grow lighter and lighter. She swiveled in her chair and stared at her red eyes in the dusky mirror and the tears on her cheeks and Janet Sue. She turned back and looked.

Janet Sue hugged Chloe for a long time while they watched the sunrise, long enough for all of Chloe's tears to dry and the terrible aching in her heart to stop hurting.

"You should talk to Katie," the angel said.

"Why?"

"This is the reason she is here."

Chloe tilted her head back to look directly at the loving eyes.

"I love how you talk to me without moving your lips. You did that when I was eight, too. You are my precious angel."

Side by side, staring out the open window, they watched the flickering golden light glisten on the salt water waves.

"I promised I wouldn't tell."

Janet Sue kissed Chloe on her forehead.

"You talk to Katie soon. I'll take care of your promise."

●●●

The men gathered around the green metal table in the Quonset hut on Airfield San Antonio de los Baños, Havana.

Quinn pushed the replay message button on the cell phone discovered in the cathedral bell tower.

"The list just got longer," is all the phone message said.

"Well, that sounds like a declaration of war," Vincent Bonifacio declared.

"Sure does," Quinn agreed.

"At least they don't have any damn infected mosquitoes now," Richard said.

Quinn looked at Richard.

"Let's you and I take a road trip."

"Where?"

"Suriname, Paramaribo, Fort Willoughby to be precise. Juan Castro has tracked Robert Cash's boat to that location twice in the past month. I love GPS. Let's be his welcoming committee."

"Let's," Richard grinned.

"I'm going to Big Bay, Quinn, with Timothy. Keep an eye on things there."

"Good idea, Vincent."

CHAPTER 40

ONE PLANTED CELL PHONE

Robert Cash fears flying; terrified, actually – absolute fear – since watching the earth coming up rapidly, spinning around and around and, finally, a palm tree plunging through the helicopter windshield. The crash killed six of his fellow Green Berets and rendered him unconscious for three weeks on a naval hospital ship cruising the coast of South Vietnam.

He travels mostly by car or train. Whenever possible, he travels on water in his favorite boat. He named the boat *Alli*, after a lady he met in Saigon and had hoped to marry. After his helicopter crash, he never returned to the war and never saw Alli again. He longingly named his Scarab in memory of his unfulfilled love.

Time has not helped. Even the percussive chopping sounds of helicopter blades slicing through the air tense Robert's body, his mind involuntarily reliving the spinning earth coming closer...closer...closer and bracing for the crunching, metallic grinding.

It had been a close call. If the corporal in charge of the refueling truck loaded with jet fuel had not overheard Quinn O'Malley and the XS-1 pilots calculating the fuel needed for a round trip to Nicaragua, they would have caught him in the sanctuary of Cathedral San Pedro.

Robert Cash had traveled over the Caribbean Sea in his Scarab from Paramaribo, Suriname to La Barra, Nicaragua. The trip took twenty-six hours. He liked being alone, listening to the harmonic sounds of the twin 500 horsepower engines. At La Barra, he entered the river's mouth and went up the Rio Grande de Matagalpa to the city of Matagalpa.

Angry, Robert intended to get answers about the mosquito problem and had a meeting scheduled with the lead scientists for Thursday morning. He had closed his eyes for about ten minutes, lying on a cot in a little room across from the confessional, when he received the call from Cuba.

"They have launched the stealth helicopter on a mission to Nicaragua," the corporal's voice said. "It will take two hours before they arrive."

"Thank you."

Robert quickly walked up the stairs and placed a cell phone on the window ledge. Then he ran into the darkness as fast as his limping left leg would allow to the boathouse on the riverbank. He flipped the switch activating the ventilation fans and waited, listening, panting.

…I sound like a wheezing fox hound…

Then he started the port engine and backed out of the boathouse, heading east down the river.

The chopping sounds of the helicopter, even though distant, tensed Robert, every muscle quivering. He felt cold.

…watch the banks…careful…damn O'Malley…

He slowed the racing boat to a crawl, just fast enough to control the steering, and called the cell phone on the window ledge. He let it ring for several minutes before leaving a terse message.

The sky lit up behind him. He turned his head to watch and listen. The echoing sound of the explosion…the bluish yellow flashes in the sky.

…Mekong Delta…they're here…the regulars are here…

Robert Cash stared at the flickering sky with wide angry eyes.

He reached into his pants pocket for his phone and called Ivan.

"Meeting next Monday. Everyone there. Next Monday. Noon."

"Yes, sir."

"The war has started."

CHAPTER 41

MOTHERS PROTECT THEIR BABIES

Timothy and Vincent stood watching in the darkness from Union Street, looking through Poor Joe's open front door at Machete sitting just inside on a chair. Little Miss sat at his side. They watched patrons walking up the concrete steps and through the open door. Little Miss barked once with the approach of each customer; Machete greeted each with a smile, holding his hand out.

"What the hell?" Timothy said.

"Looks to me like you've got a greeter, Timothy."

"This ought to be fun," Timothy said. They walked across the street toward the steps.

Little Miss started licking Machete's arm.

"Hi, Timothy." Machete extended his right hand.

"What *are* you doing?"

"Moses promoted me to greeter. I'm in charge of greeting our customers. I get paid in meals."

"Machete, your meals were already free."

"Now I earn them. They taste even more delicious. Hello, Vincent!"

"How'd you know I'm here?"

"The same Italian aftershave you've always used."

Norah Chase rolled over and rubbed her eyes, looking again at the wooden chair next to her bedroom vanity.

*…I loved that dream…*she thought, watching the dust shadows floating down the west wall. The soft beam of morning sunshine from the high window on the east wall illuminated her bedroom.

*…it tickled when she touched me…*imagining the slender young lady in her dream. Norah even imagined she smelled the sweet fragrances of the long blond hair when the lady bent over and kissed her on the forehead.

*…oooh…St. Kitts!…St. Kitts!…*Wire-Rim pulled her hair in St. Kitts…

Then Norah rolled to her back and stared at the ceiling. She rubbed her belly and wondered.

• • •

"Fort Willoughby is nearly impenetrable without casualties," Quinn said to Richard, "to answer your question."

"Thought it would be easier to do a fly-by and share a rocket."

"The Suriname Air Force has two F-14's in the air over Paramaribo, twenty-four hours a day. There's a Russian-built destroyer with surface-to-air missiles just offshore. A full regiment of Presidential Special Forces are stationed in Paramaribo."

"That's impressive," Richard replied, walking in the darkness with Quinn, along the Suriname riverbank. "Guess we don't want to cause an international incident."

"It's under the guise of presidential protection. Come to find out, His Excellency, the minister of defense, is on The Company's payroll; just a little fact disclosed on the red thumb drive. The surplus F-14's and naval vessels are gifts to Suriname in the name of security. In exchange, The Company has the use of Fort Willoughby."

"How convenient," Richard said. "How we gonna get in?"

"Have an association with one of the guards. He's disabled the second floor air conditioner. We are the repairmen. He has a panel truck waiting for us at the intersection of Wilhelminastraat and Mahonylaan streets."

"You know anything about fixing air conditioners?"

"The missing fuses are in the glove compartment. He's left jumpsuits for us. We'll be in uniform, Richard; piece of cake."

Richard grinned his crooked grin in the darkness.

"I've agreed to get the guard's cousin and his family out of the country for the use of his truck."

"Seems only fair. This is going to be fun."

•••

The white panel truck with AIR CONDITIONING REPARATIE in bold black lettering on each side came to a stop in front of the fort caretaker's two story house at twelve-fifteen. The guards on the front porch and the second story balcony pointed their automatic weapons at the vehicle.

"HALTE!" the ranking guard shouted in Dutch from the front porch, recognizing his cousin's work truck.

"Air conditioner *reparatie*," Quinn replied.

Snipers from their positions on the second story balcony peered at Quinn and Richard's heads through their scopes.

"Godzidank!" (Thank God!) the guard replied, lowering his weapon and waving to the other guards to do likewise.

Quinn, followed by Richard carrying a red metal tool chest, walked up the narrow wooden stairs.

A young guard standing just inside the second story door turned and faced them. He racked his automatic rifle and moved the safety to the off position.

"Air conditioner *reparatie*," Quinn said.

"About time." Robert Cash studied the men in white jumpsuits. He wiped the perspiration from his forehead.

Richard smiled while placing the tool chest on the floor, gently, next to the window air conditioner. He opened the tool chest, reached in and as everyone in the room watched, lifted a pistol equipped with a silencer and shot the guard once in the forehead.

Ivan Khrushchev twisted around, looking back toward Richard, and then back at Quinn.

"Quinn O'Malley!" Ivan growled. He reached into his jacket pocket, pulling a pistol from the lining holster. Extending his right arm toward Quinn, he squeezed the trigger of a small handgun.

Quinn flinched.

Richard shot Ivan twice.

"Anyone else want to play hero?" Richard spoke in a voice barely audible. He watched Quinn's face.

"You'll never get out of here," Robert said with disdain.

"That's what you thought about us getting in here, I'll bet," Quinn said.

Robert glared.

"Hey, Quinn, you want I just shoot the rest of 'em and we get the hell out of here?"

Quinn winked at Richard.

"Quinn O'Malley, we finally meet. And, Richard Elmore Fortin…I recognize your face…an instant television celebrity. What do you guys want?"

"We want you to stop," Quinn said. "Simple, Robert, we want you to get out of business – you and Raul over there, and John, you too, and Hector, and you too, Jimmy from China. We want you out of business."

Raul fidgeted with the cell phone in his pocket.

Jimmy smiled a sardonic smile and shuffled papers over and over. He glanced at Robert, dark anger in his eyes.

"Is that all? Why no problem; right boys? You got it, Quinn," Robert said, looking at dead Ivan, his head lying on the table.

"Figured you'd see it our way," Quinn said.

"Now what?" Robert asked.

Raul, as inconspicuously as he could manage, extended two fingers of his right hand into his pants pocket.

"All your cell phones on the table…everyone. Please don't disappoint Richard here; he's not mentally stable these days."

The cell phones clattered on the table.

"And now your weapons; right, Richard?"

Richard made a crazy distorted face, accentuating the scar on his right cheek, and nodded yes.

Robert slid a pistol on the table. So did Raul. The others raised their hands, claiming no weapons.

"Stand!" he commanded, and he patted down Hector, John, and Jimmy.

"You gonna die," Hector sneered.

"Counting on it," Quinn replied. "Crazy Richard has on at least two occasions; claims it's not bad."

"OK! Now, Robert, you may adjourn this meeting of The Company. There will not be another meeting."

"You have my word," Robert sneered.

"Let me hold your pistol while you change, crazy Richard," Quinn said. "Then I'll change."

Richard peeled off the white workman's jumpsuit, revealing a crisp Suriname military uniform. He took the pistol back from Quinn while Quinn did the same.

Richard looked at the small hole in Quinn's jumpsuit and smiled, relieved the white cloth had no red.

"OK then, Robert Cash, let's go for a boat ride."

"What?" Robert Cash replied.

Richard screwed his face up again. "You just gonna let them go?"

"In England, we always gave the fox a fair start, a bit of a head start, before we turned the hounds loose. Seems only right, crazy Richard, don't you think?"

"Checkmate!" Richard replied.

"Now, gentlemen, let's all go for a walk to the marina," Quinn said. "You and your buddies will get on Alli and head out to God knows where, far, far away. Never, ever do I want to hear you're alive again."

The five men came down the stairs, following Quinn. Richard followed, last in the line – five men dressed in white tropical suits and two men in crisp green military uniforms – walking together down the sidewalk toward the marina while the guards on the porches watched.

The guards on the front porch saluted the two uniformed officers walking past them. Quinn and Richard returned the salutes.

"Be sure to turn the ventilation fans on," Quinn said, watching the five men climb aboard the Scarab. "Wouldn't want an explosion."

Richard and Quinn watched the rumbling Scarab leave the marina toward the mouth of the river.

"Crazy Richard? Really, Quinn? Mentally unstable?"

Quinn laughed. "You should have seen their eyes."

"How far they gonna get?"

"Not far. Robert will head for the destroyer. He thinks it's his sanctuary. Not far."

Richard looked at Quinn.

"Destroyers don't like being attacked by Scarabs – terrorists, rebels, such as that – on our high seas."

Quinn smiled.

"I'm acquainted with the admiral aboard. His father went to college with Fidel and me. Now, let's go find out how Robert knew we were on our way to Nicaragua."

"I didn't know you knew Dutch."

"Picked up a few words in Amsterdam years ago."

"Hurt much, where Ivan shot you?"

"Not bad. These new vests do a good job. Feels like rib number five might be cracked. I like that they're not hot; like wearing a T-shirt."

"Stanley will tape it when we get back."

They walked along listening to the tiny sea shells crunch underfoot before they began wading in the warm saltwater until they reached a rubber dinghy hidden in the reeds. Richard paddled out several hundred feet towards a periscope peeking up.

Quinn tapped several times against the metal with a stick.

"The Cubans are right on time."

The Cuban naval submarine hatch opened.

"I'd rather fly," Richard muttered.

● ● ●

Everyone had said goodnight after sunset, leaving Belvia and her oldest daughter alone on the red brick patio. Lina opened the sliding glass doors one last time before retiring for the night. "Can I get you ladies anything before I go to bed?" she asked.

"I'm fine; you, Norah?"

"Hot cocoa; I'd like hot cocoa with marshmallows on top."

"I'll be right back," Lina said. "That gonna keep you up tonight, sweetie."

"You're growing up to be a beautiful young lady, Norah," Belvia said. "I was never as beautiful as you are, when I was a teenager."

Norah skooched down in her chair and brought her knees up, resting her chin.

"What's wrong, sweetheart?"

Norah shrugged, shaking her head back and forth.

"When I allow my mind to think about the horror you went through, I cry, too. I would have changed places with you in a heartbeat. Mothers protect their babies, no matter what or how old; that's what mothers do. They protect their babies. I am so sorry."

They sat silently, listening to the crickets.

Lina opened the door, bringing a marshmallow-crowned mug of hot chocolate. She stopped partway to the table and paused, watching the teenager with her chin resting on her knees, her eyes welling up and Belvia on the verge of tears.

"I gonna say an extra prayer for you guys tonight," Lina said in broken English.

"Thank you, Lina," Belvia said, reaching her hand back and grasping Lina's hand. "Your English is getting better each day."

"That Miss Chloe be a good teacher!" Lina replied.

"Want a sip, Mom?"

Norah pushed the mug across the table, spilling one marshmallow on the glass tabletop halfway between them.

Belvia sipped the cocoa and asked, "Anything I can do to make things better?"

Norah took a deep breath and wiped at her nose with the back of her hand.

"I haven't had a period in almost three months, mom."

…oh shit…my poor baby…please help us Jesus…help…not this too…

"We don't know for sure, Norah. You've been under a lot of stress the past three months. We don't know for sure. How 'bout we ask Doctor Blue to check you over?"

"He knows I got raped right before we were rescued."

Mother and daughter sat without saying a word for a long time. Lina watched for a while through the sliding glass doors and then said a prayer and crossed herself before going down to her bedroom.

CHAPTER 42

ON HIGH AUTHORITY

"Does her mother know?" Katie asked, walking next to Chloe on the path leading from the brick patio toward Dora Castro's favorite tropical flower garden.

"I think I'm the only one, and I promised. It's a secret. She told me last week when we took turns driving my car. I promised, Katie. I feel awful right now telling you."

"Why are you?"

"Janet Sue said to."

Katie smiled and kinda shrugged.

"I've met her, you know."

"I know, Mom said you met her that time you were praying for me in the hospital."

They stopped while Chloe picked two flowers. She handed a red flower to Katie and snuggled a yellow blossom into the hair above her right ear.

"That's why, cuz I knew you wouldn't think I'm nuts and because she told me to talk to you."

"How long since her last period, Chloe? Did she say?"

"Two months, almost three. She's so scared."

"What happened?"

"The man who gave her drugs every night raped her. He said if she told anybody, even Doctor Blue, he would kill them both."

Chloe wiped at her cheeks.

"She told Doctor Blue anyway. He made her promise to tell

absolutely no one else. No one could know because she had been sold to a rich prince who wanted only virgins and if the prince found out, he would refuse her, and they would sell her to the next highest offer. Can you believe it, Katie? Can you believe it…these evil people?"

"I have never understood evil, Chloe. It's the first thing I'm going to ask when I get to heaven, right after I hug Doug and say hi to Jesus. I'm going to ask, 'Why the evil? Why didn't you just blot it out? There're other ways we could've made our choices; we didn't need evil hurting the innocent ones."

"Wow, and you're a lawyer and preacher; I thought you'd know."

"I'm clueless, Chloe. But I hate it."

"Me, too."

They stopped walking at a bench overlooking the water and sat, watching the tiny waves sparkle far below.

"Norah hasn't said a word to Belvia about this?"

"I don't think so. Doctor Blue knows she was raped, but she hasn't told him this."

Katie held Chloe's left hand.

"I try to imagine how awful I would feel if that had been me," Chloe said, looking at Katie. "I try to put myself in her place and I just start crying. I know it's wrong, but I'd ask Richard to go kill that man and I know he would; for me he would. I think about it at night, asking him to do it for Norah."

Katie smiled. She put her arm around Chloe and squeezed her close.

"I believe he would, honey. Richard has an impeccable sense of justice. He loves his friends absolutely."

Chloe looked at Katie's face and said, "I can imagine him as the lead horseman of the apocalypse."

Katie smiled. "I guess I can, too. How do you know this stuff?"

"One of my Spanish lessons was to read "The Revelations" in Spanish. I don't understand most of it, but I sure can picture the four horsemen."

"I'm in the same boat, Chloe. Here's a secret, OK?"

"Promise…double promise," Chloe said.

"Quinn's wife shot that man the day the True Believers rescued A.W. and Norah. He's dead."

"Debra shot him!"

"I have it on high authority, that bad man is dead. Ask Norah; she watched it happen."

They both felt a gentle hand on their backs at the same instant. Twisting backward, they looked at Norah's flushed face.

"Hi, Norah, we were just talking about you," Katie said.

"I know." She climbed over the bench and squeezed between them. "I've been listening for a while."

"I'm sorry…trying to have Katie help us. Sorry I broke my promise."

"I started my period this morning…really hard."

"Yay!" Chloe yelled.

Katie turned her head to the right, watching the young ladies surround each other with their arms, their faces touching, wet cheek to wet cheek.

…thank you, Jesus…

"What does that Janet Sue look like?"

"Long blond hair, and her eyes glow with love," Chloe answered.

"Who is she?"

"Janet Sue is Wendell's high school sweetheart. She died in a car accident," Katie replied. "Wendell hit a tree on the way home from a high school dance."

"She came to St. Kitts. Janet Sue helped us escape. I've seen her! And I had a dream about her."

"That wasn't a dream, Norah. She told me to tell Katie. She's here, helping us."

Norah leaned forward and whimpered a little groan.

"This one really hurts."

Katie smiled, watching the two teenagers chatting.

"Mom wants for me to have a checkup with Doctor Blue," Norah said between grimaces.

"Your mom knows?" Chloe asked.

"We talked last night before we went to bed."

"Let's get you back up to the house, Norah. I think we should have Doctor Blue check now."

"OK, this really hurts."

CHAPTER 43

THE MOST PRECIOUS THING

Quinn, Richard, and Stanley sat on the patio, drinking coffee, watching Katie, Chloe and Norah walk slowly up the path through the flower gardens toward them.

"What time did you guys get here?" Stanley poured extra cream in the dark coffee.

"Five this morning," Quinn replied.

"Do I dare ask where you've been?"

"South America," Richard replied. "Ever been to Suriname?"

Stanley grinned. "I have not."

"Don't go."

"OK."

"Your daughter and Norah are becoming beautiful young ladies, Stan," Quinn commented. "I've got a daughter, in Miami, last I knew. That was years ago. That's on the top of my failure list."

Stanley twisted so he could look directly at his old friend.

"It's not too late to rectify that, you know."

"Scares the crap out of me, Stan."

Quinn reached in his pocket and retrieved his yellow Comstat phone.

"Hi, Vincent, how's the olive oil convention?"

"A great success. All quiet here. How're things down there?"

"Just received confirmation forty minutes ago, a Suriname Navy destroyer came across a pirate boat running drugs and sank it."

"Good news, Quinn. One more night in Big Bay, and we'll end

the convention before I go broke. The guys love it here, and Timothy is getting rich. Have you met his new cook?"

"If you're talking about Moses, just briefly; helped with her citizenship papers."

"That's her. Poor Joe's isn't the same. You'll like her."

"First lady I've met named Moses." Quinn chuckled.

"I've never met a lady quite like her, trust me. Neither has Machete; he's smitten."

"Thanks, Vincent, for looking after the place. We'll be in touch, my friend."

● ● ●

Doctor A.W. Blue opened the white door with a little red cross in the center and walked out from the presidential medical clinic on the lower level of the compound, stocked for any eventuality by Doctor Gonzales.

Through the open door, those waiting could see Norah lying on a cot, covered by a white sheet, with Belvia sitting beside her.

"Spontaneous abortion. Norah's had a miscarriage," the old doctor said. "Danielle and I did a D&C. Norah's going to be fine."

He looked at Chloe.

"Sometimes life's a bitch, ain't it, honey?"

"Yes, doctor."

"The most precious things in this life are genuine friends. Never forget, Chloe, the most precious things, right, Katie?"

"Absolutely," Katie replied.

Danielle walked through the clinic door and embraced her daughter tightly for a long time.

"Now, go be with your friend. She needs you."

After Chloe left, Katie said to Danielle, "Your daughter is a gift from God."

"I know," Danielle said. Then she grinned. "She invite you to her Spanish classes yet?"

"No."

"She will."

"I'll go. I wish I understood life the way she already does at age sixteen."

CHAPTER 44

NO QUESTIONS ASKED

W hen she was twenty-one, Rose won in all categories and became the state of New York's representative to the Miss America Pageant. A stunningly vivacious young lady, Miss New York looked forward to winning Miss America and traveling. The night after her New York crowning, one of the judges invited her on a tour of New York City and to dinner. Rose does not recall much of the evening after dinner, excepting that the man seduced her.

The following morning Rose stood on a bridge and dropped her queen's crown into the Hudson River. She left New York City following a call to her Uncle Robert in Reno, Nevada. Rose did not participate in the Miss America Pageant in Atlantic City.

Now a stunning sixty-year-old with dyed, red hair, Rose simply smiles when gentlemen hit on her. She owns a casino in Vegas and two gentlemen's clubs in Reno. A tolerant and empathic soul, she will tolerate most behavior except for dishonesty and lies.

Frequently, she has been known to throw men out of her gentlemen's clubs after asking the men if they were married.

"Are you a married man?" she will ask customers.

When the startled men reply *yes*, she asks, "Does your wife know you're here?"

When the reply is sarcastic, "Of course not," she has the bouncers throw them out, saying, "No cheaters or liars in my house." When the answer is a tentative *yes*, she instructs the men to come back with a "permission note" from their wives.

"Everyone needs to feel close, to feel that human touch," she replies when her line of work is criticized by the various religious groups searching for a cause. "But I'll not be a party to cheatin' and lies."

She met Vincent Bonifacio in Vegas twenty years ago through her Uncle Robert. They became close friends immediately. Vincent introduced Rose to his old friend, Quinn O'Malley. Not long after that meeting, Rose began to help finance the True Believers.

She refused to even date men until she met one of the Usual Suspects named Jonathon at Poor Joe's. She took him back to Reno with her and married the only man she had truly loved on the day she turned fifty.

Years after the incident in New York City, the pageant judge disappeared. Nine days later his body washed ashore in Atlantic City. Quinn shared the news with his new friend, Rose, on her birthday.

●●●

"They sure are a close-knit bunch," Amy Hamilton said to Rose. The two women sat on the brick patio, watching the people through the large windows gathered outside the medical clinic door. Danielle had just hugged Chloe.

Rose stayed at the Cuban compound while Quinn and Richard left on a "mission," and Vincent had left with Timothy to keep an eye on things in Big Bay. "Someone needs to keep an eye on Amy, and between Deb and me, we've got her covered. We're just the girls for the job," she had told Quinn, who smiled and nodded yes.

"You don't understand them, do you?" Rose asked.

"Not really," Amy answered

"It's called love, Amy. They truly care deeply. They care and they'll do anything to help each other, no questions asked."

"Oh. Still don't get it."

"I have no trouble believing that."

"What does that mean?"

"That means," Rose said, "that a selfish person cannot understand love."

"You're taking a shot at me, right?"

"Well, I've never thought you were stupid, just selfish."

"What line of work are you in?" Amy asked, with a hint of sarcasm.

"I'm in the entertainment business, helping lonely people feel less lonely."

"I heard you run a whorehouse."

Rose smiled at Amy.

"I hear you need a job."

CHAPTER 45

AIN'T IT BEAUTIFUL!

"Will you marry me?"

Moses held both of Machete's hands, reaching across the table top in the corner booth, next to the popcorn machine, now silent because Poor Joe's had closed for the night.

She stared at his dark, blind, glistening eyes.

"You do not even know me, Machete Juarez."

"I know that I love you."

"I love you, too."

"I know that you have a kind soul. I know that you love living. I know that there is nothing I will not do for you, to bring you joy and happiness. That is what I know…and that you are a beautiful person."

Moses stood and walked to Machete's side of the booth.

"Slide over."

She slid close.

"I been wit many men dat wanted me…," Moses said, her chin almost touching Machete's shoulder. "I heard dat once you lived de life of a ghetto alley cat. I know what dat life be like, Machete."

"The past is not worth the effort it takes to remember," Machete said, moving closer and closer. "What I know is that you are here from Guadeloupe and I am here from Mexico City, and those places do not matter in our lives anymore except to be thankful we are here together in Big Bay. And no accident, I think."

"I will marry you! I like de sound of dat name…Moses Juarez!"

For the first time, Moses and Machete kissed.

Then they sat in the corner booth for a long time, their heads bowed, holding each other tightly.

"I'm gonna love you forever," Machete finally said.

"I know," Moses replied. "Dat's how love works."

●●●

"I gonna miss all dose Italian boys," Moses said to Timothy.

She finished grinding the coffee and took a pan of apple croissants out of the oven.

"Yes sir, dey be friendly and tip real big."

Timothy smiled.

"Machete asked me to marry him."

"He did!"

"Last night, after closing."

"What'd you say?"

"I say I like da sound of Moses Juarez. I say yes, silly man."

"Congratulations!"

The door under the stairs opened. Machete and Little Miss walked into the bar.

"Mornin,' Machete," Timothy said. He turned on the TV.

"Good morning, Timothy. Hi, honey."

Moses giggled a little giggle.

"She told you, didn't she?"

"I'm thrilled for you guys." Timothy walked over to Machete and placed his hand on the little Mexican's shoulder.

Looking at Moses in the kitchen, he continued, "You guys have my best wishes for much happiness and much love in your lives together."

"Thank you," Moses and Machete said in unison.

"When you getting married?"

"Do you know when Katie will be back?" Machete asked.

"I think Katie is going to be gone for quite a while. Judge Linsenmayer can marry you," Timothy replied.

"Well, let's call her!" Moses said. "She be up by now?"

Timothy grinned. "You in a hurry? You're not pregnant are you?" he said, handing his phone to Moses after entering the judge's phone number and pushing the call button.

"Oh, Mister Timothy, we just kissed for de first time last night. Ain't it beautiful, how love makes you feel!"

"It is for a fact, Moses, it is for a fact."

Timothy walked back to Machete, sitting at the small round table in the southwest corner. He leaned down close to Machete's left ear and whispered, "Moses is one of the most beautiful ladies I have ever seen, all the way to her soul. You're a lucky man."

"I know that already."

"What you men be whispering 'bout?" Moses shouted from the kitchen.

Machete laughed.

"She say yes!" Moses exclaimed, waving Timothy's cell phone high and dancing around the kitchen. "Da judge say yes; just let her know when and I say tomorrow at ten!"

Moses danced to an imaginary reggae band closer and closer toward Timothy and the man she knew she loved from the very first time she saw him sitting alone stroking Little Miss on her head.

CHAPTER 46

OLD SCHOOL MOVE

Admiral José Dorta watched the Scarab racing toward his naval destroyer. The racing boat disappeared into the valleys and sometimes the patchy fog, reappearing, coming closer and closer at seventy knots, leaving the water briefly on the waves' crests. He ordered his ship to come to a complete stop and waited. When the Scarab pulled alongside the Suriname destroyer, several sailors tossed a rope ladder over the port side, lowering it to the bobbing little boat.

Five men, led by Robert Cash, climbed the ropes. The sailors helped them when they reached the railing.

Then the destroyer backed away from the Scarab. At 100 yards, the Suriname sailors used the racing boat for target practice before using a cannon and blowing *Alli* into tiny pieces.

Robert Cash watched for a brief period then turned away. He walked to the bridge.

"Thank you for providing asylum, Admiral."

"His Excellency the president sends his regards and continued appreciation of your support, Robert Cash."

"Tell His Excellency I am grateful."

"What happened at Fort Willoughby?"

"Ambushed by my old nemesis, Quinn O'Malley, and his crazy sidekick, Richard Elmore Fortin."

"How did they get past security?"

"Air-conditioner repairmen. Dammit. Can you believe it? They got past security dressed as air conditioner repairmen. Fortin shot our upstairs guard and then Ivan before marching us down to the marina – son of a bitch – in a line like prisoners of war."

"You are fortunate to be alive, still," the admiral said.

"Quinn O'Malley plays life like a chess match. Didn't see that move coming – old school move – from a guy with unbelievable high tech toys. Old school. I'm better, Admiral…I'm better. I'll win the match."

"What's your next move?"

"I'll let you know."

"My father went to University of Habana with O'Malley and Castro. I remember him in my youth."

"O'Malley is counting on his past alliance with your father. I am sure he believes your destroyer eliminated my Scarab."

Admiral José Dorta looked out the window, watching cushions and bits of fiberglass floating on the saltwater.

"It did," he replied. "And I sent the radio message."

•••

"Hey, Stanley, want to hear the latest from Big Bay?" Timothy spoke into his yellow Comstat phone, looking at the newlyweds.

"Sure! Wait just a second; I'll get everyone close. I'm putting you on speaker mode."

Danielle, A.W. Blue, Quinn, Richard, Chloe, Katie, Norah, and Belvia huddled around the table outside. Belvia's youngest, Edmund, joined them with a handful of Lina's pastries.

"Faith just married Moses and Machete."

Danielle, Katie, and Belvia began clapping and then, too, did Chloe and Norah.

"How wonderful. Tell them we are thrilled for them."

"You just did."

"Way to go, Machete!" Richard shouted in the direction of the phone.

"Thanks, Richard. Your turn now, my amigo. You and Belvia next."

"She's standing right here, Machete."

"Good, just helping," Machete said. And they could hear him chuckling in the background.

Moses reached for Timothy's phone.

"Mister Timothy has given us de most wonderful wedding gift!" Moses exclaimed. "You can never guess in a million years, I bet."

"You're right, and I don't have a million years, so tell us," Quinn said.

"Mister Timothy gave us Poor Joe's. He said, 'Here be my wedding gift to you guys from all of us who love dis old bar and from all of dose who have ever loved her. Congratulations and best wishes.' Dat be exactly what he said to us. Can you believe it?"

The people huddled around the glass table on the patio in Nueva Gerona stared at each other then broke out with clapping and cheering.

"You gonna love da food when you finally come back home," Moses said. "Sorry, Mister Timothy, no disrespect."

Timothy laughed. "She's right! Hey, Quinn, you there?"

"Go ahead."

"Wendell said he would look after things and keep the crockpot filled with chili. Thought Carla and I might bring Moses and Machete down for a little getaway – honeymoon for the newlyweds and a vacation for the Fifes."

"Superior idea, Timothy. When would you like the plane?"

"Next Monday."

"It'll be there at 10:00."

"Oh, is Chloe with you guys right now?"

"I'm here!" Chloe said loudly at the phone lying in the middle of the table.

"Charles is coming, too."

Chloe blushed and glanced at Norah and then her mother.

CHAPTER 47

LEAD HORSEMAN OF THE APOCALYPSE

"I love living here," Danielle said to Stanley. "I have absolutely no desire to go home right now."

"Me neither. That last round with Tiffany soured me; I truly don't want to walk back through those hospital doors. Ramona just retired. Jack McCaferty is retiring next month and so is Laverne Smith."

Stanley paused, watching the sunrise with his wife.

"All of the nurses that were there when I hired on are gone. It's just not the same."

Danielle twisted around and faced her husband.

"All of the nurses you've hired over the years are mostly there, and they love you."

The sun rose higher. The waves glistened bright and they both put on sunglasses.

"But, not as much as I love you." And Danielle gave Stanley a quick kiss on his cheek. "And I want to keep you around for a bunch more years, old man, so if retiring from Big Bay General will help, I say let's."

"Chloe seems right at home in Cuba. I watched her last week, walking with her classmates, speaking in Spanish, laughing, and I had no idea what they were saying, but she just beamed. And then I watch her and Norah together, driving around in the VW; they seem right at home," Stanley said, pouring more coffee into their cups.

"That's been intriguing," Danielle said.

"What's intriguing?"

"Watching our daughter. She has taken Norah under her wing just like my grandmother Lagasse did with me after my mother left us, like an old grandma, loving her and protecting her and making her laugh. Now they only communicate in Spanish. I asked Chloe why and she told me because all the bad stuff happened in English and that Spanish is happier and besides, it's sexier, too."

"Oh brother."

"She's excited that Charles Fife is coming down, I can tell you that."

"She gonna find someone for Norah so they can double date while he's here?"

"You know she is, Stan."

"Wonder how Norah will feel about dating."

"I asked Chloe about that. She gave me one of her quick grins and said, 'Oh Mom, we'll all speak in Spanish and laugh a lot at our mistakes.'"

"Charlie Fife is going to speak in Spanish?"

"Chloe's been giving him lessons for the past year."

"Oh brother."

"You're still at the top of her list, Stan."

"So she'll be OK if we don't go back?"

"I think she feels the same way about it as we do. She would like to have Amy Hamilton disappear, though."

"I'm leaving that up to Quinn and Richard. They brought her here."

"Chloe mentioned that and then something about the lead horsemen of the Apocalypse, whatever that means, and she laughed."

Stanley's mind percolated through unused memories and past theological studies.

…the Four Horsemen of the Apocalypse…

"The lead horseman of the Apocalypse rode a white horse, Danielle."

She smiled an admiring smile. "You would know that."

"In Revelations the first horseman rode a white horse, symbolizing conquest," Stanley said. "I can see Richard Elmore Fortin riding that horse."

"So can your daughter."

CHAPTER 48

NEVER WRONG

The explosive concussion bowed the hurricane garage doors inward at the Conch Republic Seafood Company. The remains of the fishing charter boats tethered in Key West Marina slips #9 and #10 hurdled through the air, bouncing on the Commodore Waterfront Restaurant deck. Some boat pieces shattered the windows at the adjacent A&B Lobster House and White Tarpon Deli.

At 3:33 on a Sunday morning, *Key West Dreamer,* Quinn O'Malley's beloved old boat, tethered in the Key West marina at slip #8, exploded.

The early morning staff, preparing for breakfast at the Schooner Wharf, felt the concussion all the way across the marina.

•••

The sound of a large brown helicopter landing on the villa helipad awakened everyone.

Stanley watched Quinn O'Malley walk down the lighted pathway on the gentle slope toward the helicopter. The side door opened, and in the early morning dusk, he watched Quinn and Fidel embrace. Fidel then held his old friend at arm's length and spoke earnestly for several minutes. The two elderly men left the helipad, walking up the slope toward the compound, stopping only once to watch two C-130 transport planes flying in the direction of the airport.

Lina carried two large pitchers of dark coffee to the outdoor patio table and then returned with a tray of cups, a small pitcher of cream, and a saucer of brown sugar cubes.

Stanley joined Fidel and Quinn. Quickly, and almost silently, the chairs around the round glass table filled. Richard, A.W., Debra, and Rose. Lastly, Danielle walked through the sliding glass patio doors and closed them behind her.

"I know I'm not usually part of this group," Danielle said, pulling over another chair and squeezing in next to Stanley, "but I was there in Cardenas; I've been with you when…" She paused and looked up at Katie opening the sliding door.

Katie picked up and carried a chair to the table. She sat next to Fidel.

"Will Dora be joining us?" she asked the president of Cuba.

"Soon." He reached out and patted Katie's hand. "Soon."

Stanley noticed Quinn's very pale complexion, even in the early morning light.

"They blew up my boat," Quinn said. *"Key West Dreamer is gone."*

Richard shivered, remembering his introduction to Quinn O'Malley, sitting on the *Key West Dreamer's* wooden deck in the darkness.

…you following me for any particular reason? looking up from his boat. I don't know…you don't know if you are following me, or you don't know if you have a reason? Come aboard, young fellow, and introduce yourself, Richard Elmore Fortin…

Danielle stared down the slope at the brown helicopter, the rotors turning slower and slower.

…watching Mallory Square in the distance disappearing in the morning fog from the stern of the Key West Dreamer…*I love you, Stanley…on our way to Cuba for the first time, riding with a crazy man we met in The Green Parrot Bar…pregnant with Chloe…we got married on the* Key West Dreamer…*Captain Quinn married us on the* Key West Dreamer…

Stanley watched Danielle's face and knew. He held her hand. It felt cold.

"Who?" Richard asked.

Fidel handed Richard several eight-by-ten black and white pictures.

"We had one of our choppers do a quick fly-over and take these from 20,000 feet," Quinn said. "An F-14 flew directly over them. They thought they were goners for a minute."

Richard glared at the pictures.

"It appears Admiral José Dorta has been bought and paid for," Quinn muttered.

"I'm happy his father is not here to see this," Fidel said sadly. "He would be very disappointed."

"So Robert Cash and The Committee got on board and then they sank the Scarab," Richard said.

"Yup. And early this morning they blew up my boat. My guard, Raul – he lives on board when I'm away – Raul is missing."

Fidel looked at Quinn.

"Raul is Fidel's nephew."

The friends sat around the table. Silently they drank coffee. Their contemplations were interrupted by the sound of large, green military vehicles driving up the highway road from Nueva Gerona. Leading the long line of vehicles, including surface-to-air missile launchers, was a single 1959 Jeep with a Cuban flag flapping from a rear bumper pole.

Fidel smiled a little smile, watching the Jeep driving closer.

"I love that old Jeep," he said, recalling the last days of the revolution and the defeat of Batista. "I love that fellow driving." He pointed at his chief of staff. "He's the greatest general I have known."

"Looks like your entire army," Katie said, watching trucks filled with troops, several tanks, and missile launchers taking positions at the base of the hill.

"One battalion," Fidel replied.

The roar from seven MiG 29 fighter jets, flying over and then circling the island, had everyone looking up.

"Our latest planes," Fidel commented.

Quinn sat and seemed far, far away. Stanley reached to his left and touched his arm.

"I'm sorry about your boat."

"Me too, Stan. She was a beautiful old boat; I'm going to miss her, and I'm going to miss Raul."

Quinn leaned back in his chair and looked into the morning sky, watching the MiGs flying in distant circles.

"Well," Quinn said, looking first at the president of Cuba and then at Richard, "it's time for checkmate. They've been given every opportunity to amend their ways, don't you think?"

"They still on the destroyer?" Richard asked.

"Everyone except for the ones who blew my boat to pieces."

"I'll go to Key West," Richard said, "and check on the status of the investigation."

He winked. "I know people in paradise."

● ● ●

"Juan, I would like you to drive Quinn and me to town," Fidel said to his chief of staff.

"Are you sure, Mister President?"

"I want some of that good pizza and to talk in the open air."

"Yes, sir," the young general replied. He walked to the parking lot next to the landing pad and started the old, green Jeep. He also spoke into a handheld radio, watching Quinn and Fidel walking down the grassy hill.

Fidel looked up at the sound of a helicopter gunship that arrived from the west and then followed their Jeep down the road.

"He's the best chief of staff I've ever had," Fidel said to Quinn.

"He's the only chief of staff you've had."

"True. Still, he's a good one."

"That he is," Quinn admitted, listening to the trailing gunship.

"The Company has connections in the U.S. government. They're already suspicious of the Nicaraguan explosion. They just haven't been able to connect the dots," Quinn said.

"I know. They've been looking for an excuse since Richard bombed the Veracruz compound."

"Taking out another country's naval ship will be considered an act of war," Quinn said, watching the gas station pass to their left.

"Chloe loves the VW," Fidel said.

"She does."

"It is likely the U.S. Congress will, at the least, impose restrictions, maybe even another embargo if they connect the dots," Quinn said.

"Maybe even declare war, if the hawks get their way, if they get proof," Fidel said.

"Still think it's worth it?" Quinn queried.

"Suriname has never owned that destroyer."

"You and I know that. The Company knows that. So, too, do the congressmen who will insist on a declaration of war against Cuba," Quinn said.

"Remember what he said," Fidel asked, pointing at Juan, "when I told him he could have been executed for deserting and blocking the road to the hospital in Cardenas?"

Quinn smiled.

"I do. He said, 'It's never wrong to do the right thing.'"

The Jeep drove slowly down 30th Street and stopped next to Pizzeria La Gondola.

Juan Castro looked back at his passengers.

"Juan, would you please go in and place an order, a variety, for the compound, to be delivered," Fidel said. "And then have them make pizzas all day and deliver them to our troops."

"Yes, Mister President."

"Then we'll go back. We have a mission to plan."

"Yes, Mister President."

"Call Richard, Quinn. Have him meet us at the helipad."

●●●

"Does the *Ghost Wing* need to slow before launching its ordinances?" Quinn asked Richard, sitting in the front passenger seat of the idling Jeep.

"Not necessary," Richard replied. "The GPS-guided missiles can be launched traveling away, regardless of speed; just can't launch forward at Mach 5."

"We want you to be the navigator on a mission tonight," Fidel said.

Richard smiled, accentuating his scarred right cheek.

"Tonight there will be a reckoning," he said.

"We're riding along," Quinn said, nodding toward his old friend.

"Wonderful."

●●●

At Mach 5, flying at 60,000 feet, the *Ghost Wing* passed the Suriname destroyer below in thirty-four minutes after leaving the secret underground Havana hangar. Fidel and Quinn sat side by side in the seats just above and behind the pilot, navigator, and co-pilot. They stared over Richard's shoulder at the video screen.

Robert Cash could not sleep for extended periods of time on the rocking ship. At 2:30 he awakened with nausea and a sense of anxiety. He walked from his cabin on the port side to the aft deck and looked behind at the dark water and the bioluminescent glowing phytoplankton, leaving a bluish wake for as far as he could see. He listened to the rhythmic rumble of the destroyer's engines and smiled at the distant roar of an F-14 patrolling the Suriname coast.

At precisely 3:00 a.m., Richard slid the protective cap aside and pushed the red button launching one GPS guided missile.

The missile hit the destroyer directly in the center, right behind the smoke stack. It exploded with a bluish flash. Two F-14 fighters banked tightly and flew over and then circled around and around, watching the ship's metal structure burn and then disappear completely. The pilots looked at their empty radar screens, circling, then asked for directions from a land-based radar station.

"Perhaps a mine, or onboard failure," one pilot radioed to the other.

Quinn and Fidel leaned forward and patted Richard on his back.

"You ever ride horses?" Quinn asked Richard through the intercom.

"Yup, I'm a farm boy," Richard replied. "My favorite was named Duke."

"What color was Duke?"

"White."

CHAPTER 49

NO STINKING GREEN CARD

Sitting next to Fidel, Quinn called Timothy on his Comstat phone.

"What, Quinn?"

"Sorry to wake you."

"It's OK, I was thinking about getting up to pee."

Quinn laughed. "Ain't getting old fun!"

"Beats the alternative, I guess. What's up?"

"Close Poor Joe's. Have Wendell, Ralph, Pete, and Wayne join you guys on the plane. Just close the bar and get everyone down here. Bring Moses and Machete."

"Got a situation, huh?"

"You could say that. I'd just feel better if my friends were here right now. I'll explain over a mojito."

"Ralph won't leave his barber shop," Timothy said.

"Probably not. I'll call him."

Timothy paused. "Deal. See you soon. Oh, tell Richard two U.S. Marshals were in Poor Joe's last Friday asking about him."

"You discern anything in particular?"

"Asking about family. Wanted to know about a grandfather and whether Richard had recently been in Tennessee. Moses had a lot of fun with them, teasing them about how Italian men tip better and that Richard's grandpa had moved to South America at the invitation of a prostitute named Mary, and last she heard Mary was pregnant."

"I'll bet that pissed them off."

"It did. They demanded her green card and she said, 'I ain't got no stinking green card.'"

"They were about to arrest her when Machete came out of their room with her citizenship papers, which made them visibly agitated, and then Machete announced, 'It don't matter either way; Moses is my legal wife; you can check with Judge Faith. Now, please leave.'"

Quinn chuckled.

"On their way out the door, Moses shouted, 'Give my regards to Marshal Dillon!' Machete asked her who Marshal Dillon is, and she told him she loved the TV reruns of *Gunsmoke* and all the guys started laughing…except the marshals."

"Well, get everyone on tomorrow's plane."

Quinn pushed the disconnect button and spoke into the plane's intercom.

"Richard, federal marshals stopped by Poor Joe's, asking about you and your grandpa."

"Really!"

"Sounds like Moses gave them fits."

"I love that girl."

"Best not say that around Machete."

"Why?"

"They just got married."

Richard laughed a muffled laugh into the intercom.

"He'd take it as a compliment, grandpa, I'd bet."

"I suppose he would, at that. They're all on their way down. You can give your theory a test."

"It'd be Little Miss I'd be worried about," Richard said. He laughed. The *Ghost Wing* circled Havana once and landed.

"She can read Machete's mind, you know."

CHAPTER 50

A CONSPIRACY

Timothy phoned Chief of Police Larry Strait on the chief's private office phone Monday morning before leaving for the Big Bay airport.

"Hi, Larry, I've closed Poor Joe's for a while. We're all headed to Cuba for Machete's honeymoon and a vacation. Would you have your patrols keep an eye on the place?"

"Nice day to go fishing, Timothy. Had a fellow say he caught two big brook trout in the river below the damn yesterday."

"You're not alone, are you?"

"That's the truth, Timothy. Have fun. Hold on a second."

"I need to excuse you gentlemen for a few minutes, personal business," Chief Strait said to the two federal marshals standing on the other side of his desk.

The marshals stared down at the chief in his chair.

Chief Strait pointed toward the door. "Close it on your way out."

"Sorry, Timothy, had to excuse two marshals from my office." "They were in Poor Joe's yesterday," Timothy replied, "asking about Richard."

"Yup, they have a warrant for his arrest. Say he's an escaped prisoner from the Franklin County Jail in Tennessee."

"You're kidding. What charges?"

"Attempted rape and contempt."

"That's nuts, well maybe not the contempt part," Timothy said.

"And they're looking for someone Richard called grandpa. Evidently this grandpa showed up in the middle of the night with a band of outlaws and overpowered the jail guards and broke Richard out. I asked if they had any surveillance pictures from the jail or jail records. They don't. Somehow everything malfunctioned and tapes erased. The only way they identified Richard was from fingerprints in his cell. They tracked him back to old Air Force records. He went by the name of John Allen Saint James from Marquette, Michigan, when they arrested him."

"That's a new one! They have no idea who grandpa is?"

"Nope, or his band of bandits. The authorities have no idea how they made their escape. Marshals said it's like they just vanished into thin air."

"Ain't that something." Timothy chuckled. "Moses told them grandpa moved to South America and lives with a prostitute named Mary."

"Safe travels my friend," Chief Strait said. "I'll keep an eye on things. Say hi to my friends; pass on my regards."

"Will do. John Allen Saint James, that's a good one."

The chief opened his office door. The marshals strutted in.

"Anything in that conversation you should share with fellow officers of the law," the shorter of the two marshals asked.

"Two things I never discuss: where I find morel mushrooms and the best fishing holes. Sorry, fellows. Anything else I can help you with?"

"We think you have a pretty good idea who this grandpa person is, Chief."

"I heard someone say a fellow people call grandpa moved to someplace in South America, that he took up with some gal named Mary."

The marshals studied Larry Strait's face while he spoke.

"When you learn more, please call us," the taller of the two said, reaching his card toward Chief Strait. He tossed it on the desk.

●●●

"He knows more than he's letting on," the shorter man said from the driver's seat of the black Crown Victoria.

"We'll get a wiretap," the taller marshal replied.

•••

The children, out for their midday recess after lunch, watched the sleek Gulfstream circle above them twice while it communicated with the Nueva Gerona control tower.

"It is like a Star Wars spaceship," the boy pushing a girl on the swing set said excitedly.

"Yeah," another boy said from the teeter-totter, impressing the young lady on the opposite end. "I hear it can go at warp speed…a zillion miles per hour!"

The occupants of the plane looked through the little windows to see a line of limousines waiting beside the terminal, several military vehicles with mounted machine guns, and a lone old, green Jeep with a Cuban flag flapping in the breeze from a shiny pole extending up from the rear bumper at the head of the procession.

Timothy and Carla watched from their seats while everyone disembarked from the plane, walking into a greeting committee consisting of the president of Cuba, his wife, Dora, Stanley and Danielle with Chloe, Belvia Chase and her children, A.W. Blue alongside Katie and her children, Quinn O'Malley and his wife, Debra, Rose Jackson, Richard Elmore Fortin, and Doctor Marco Gonzales and his wife, Marciana.

Timothy put his arm around Carla and whispered, "We are among the most fortunate people in the world." They sat watching the commotion outside through the open door.

"We are, honey." Carla smiled up at her husband. "No matter the things that happen, we are loved. No matter…no questions… just love."

…the cartel lieutenant pushed harder…closer…closer…toward the Mexican godfather…sitting at his desk opening and closing a bolt cut-

ter with red handles…baby Charles screaming…pee trickling down my legs…help us, Jesus…please save us…Quinn came through the door…

Timothy looked at Carla's face and saw her eyes welling up.

He kissed her on the lips.

"Hey, get a room!" Richard yelled from the tarmac.

Through the open door, Carla noticed her son holding Chloe's hand. She walked in front of Timothy, down the ramp, toward Fidel Castro's outstretched arms.

"Welcome back," Fidel said, shaking Timothy's hand.

The president of Cuba hugged Carla. "I hope you will sing for us tonight."

"I will be honored, Mister President."

"I have all of your recordings, you know."

"I am flattered."

"And, please, call me Fidel."

He turned back to Timothy.

"Want to ride in my Jeep?"

"Sure do."

"You lovers have the back seat. Quinn's driving. Dora refuses to ride with Quinn driving."

•••

"Looks like your entire army must be here!" Carla shouted. Her long blond hair flapped like the flag behind her, passing two tanks and a missile launcher on the highway up the hill.

Fidel laughed.

"They're just on practice maneuvers. Keeps their skills sharp."

"Oh."

She looked at Timothy.

He winked.

•••

Lina and Dora had conspired to make a Cuban feast for their guests. When Moses discovered, she insisted on helping prepare the meal. "You gonna love my desserts."

The menu, designed and printed by Chloe, was intended to cover all food preferences, including vegetarian since Chloe and Norah had just converted. It included *puerco asado* (roast pork), *bistec de palomilla* (palomilla steak), *filet de cherma* (grouper fillet), *pollo asado* (roast chicken) as well as copious sides of both white and saffron rice, red beans, black beans, green salads, and fried sweet plantains.

And for dessert Moses made several Key lime pies and three mango cheesecakes.

"You girls sure you don't want to try this chicken?" Stanley chided Chloe and Norah, waving a drumstick. "Lina makes the best in the world."

"Daddy, I'm eating healthy. Want a bite of my salad? It has plantains," Chloe responded, spearing a slice of fried plantain and waving it at her father.

Stanley looked at Charley, sitting next to his daughter with a large salad on his plate, and shook his head. "She's probably going to teach you Spanish, too."

"She already has, Mister McMillen," the young man with curly black hair and acne said.

Stanley took a bite from the chicken drumstick and smiled.

"Good thing you put in English alongside the Spanish," Pete said, "or some of us wouldn't have a clue."

Wayne smiled and said, "Don't matter to me; all this Cuban stuff is delicious."

"Well, it's a conspiracy," Stanley said, reaching for some roast pork. "She will be enrolling each of you in her Spanish classes." He nodded at his daughter.

Fidel Castro smiled and winked at Quinn.

…I love that child…

CHAPTER 51

I'LL HAVE A DOUBLE, TOO

Following dinner, the young people migrated to the outdoor patio to engage in the "Dominoes World Championship." Chloe insisted only Spanish could be spoken. Rounds of laughter made the adults smile.

The adults rode the elevator to the third floor.

"The view looking down on the city at night is breathtaking, Fidel," Danielle said, standing close to the northern glass wall.

"It reminds me of the view from your deck," Fidel walked to her. "It looks like Big Bay in the darkness, don't you think, all lit up at night?"

Stanley joined them, "It does; makes me thirsty for a Basil Hayden's!"

"Timothy," Fidel called out, "please open the bar."

Timothy grinned and marveled at the selection of liquor behind the bar.

...there's stuff here from all over the world...

"I see you have a case of Basil Hayden's and plenty of rum!" he shouted from behind the bar.

...wow...Ron Matusalem Rum...never could get it...

He pulled the cork from a bottle of Matusalem and poured a shot glass.

Fidel watched Timothy. He smiled, watching Timothy's face light up while holding the special aged Cuban rum in his mouth.

With their chosen libations, each sat at the large, round table, listening to Carla play the grand piano, singing several of her newest songs.

"Beautiful, Carla. I need that CD when it comes out," Fidel said. "Now come join us."

"I brought you a demo," she said, sliding off the bench and walking to the chair next to Timothy.

From the head of the table Fidel said, "I am relieved that you are here at this safe place." He took a sip of his mojito and nodded at Timothy.

Sitting next to his friend since their days together at University of Havana, Quinn said, "The three of us deliberated, wondering how much to share about our dilemma, and Richard said, 'Hell, their lives are just as much at risk; let's just be honest,' so here's what we're up against."

Katie took a long drink from her mojito.

…Doug's waiting…it's OK…the children…

Moses reached under the table and searched for Machete's hand.

A.W. Blue stared straight ahead.

Pete stood and walked toward the bar. He carried his empty glass and Wayne's and filled them both to the rim with Jack Daniels, leaving no room for ice.

"You guys need straws?" Stanley asked. "Just bring the bottle and two straws, Pete!"

"Sunday night," Richard said, "we flew a stealth plane – known to exist by only the German engineers that designed her and the few who built her and a handful of pilots and support personnel – we flew that plane nicknamed the *Ghost Wing* to the coast of Suriname. We hit a Suriname naval destroyer with a missile that sank it almost immediately."

Doctor Blue focused on Richard's lips while he spoke the next few sentences.

"We sank that ship because we knew the head of a worldwide cartel, known as *The Company* was on board."

"Robert Cash!" Doctor Blue exclaimed.

"Yes, A.W., Robert Cash, and the entire committee you told us ran the sex business in St. Kitts."

"Praise be to God!" the frail old man said, standing, reaching to shake Richard's hand. "Thanks be to God."

"You have cut the octopus's head away from the many legs," Machete said, squeezing his young wife's hand to the point it prickled.

"The fact of the matter is this; we have committed an act of war." Fidel said. "There are people in various governments around the world at this very moment trying to understand what happened to that ship, and would even declare war on Cuba, if they knew."

"We have disrupted their businesses and they are uncertain from which way the next blow will hit them, and that is to our advantage. I am sorry your lives have been dragged into this abyss, I am truly sorry, my friends, and the lives of your precious children," Fidel said. "I love the children."

Belvia Chase sat directly across the round table from Fidel, listening, her glistening eyes flashing.

Finally, Belvia spoke. Richard held her trembling cold hand and she spoke in a quiet, determined voice.

"As much as anyone at his table, I know what this evil can do, how it can ravage and destroy. The Mexican drug cartel sold my husband the lie…he became the Alaskan drug lord…I never suspected…it destroyed our family and now he is buried in a submarine deep in the Gulf of Mexico." She paused and looked from Katie's face to Danielle and then Debra.

"If it wasn't for your wife, Quinn, and Katie…and Danielle, flying to Anchorage and taking us away from that motel, I don't know…"

Fidel looked at Belvia without blinking, seeming recording every moment.

"The people in Big Bay took us in like family and then Richard gave us the use of his place in Key West. I had never felt this kind of caring."

She wiped at her eyes with a bar napkin.

"…and then they came and stole my Norah! They raped my precious daughter, and HAD HER FOR SALE!!! God bless you, Doctor Blue, for protecting her as best you could. I think about what you did all the time, and can't thank you enough. And then you," She said twisting her head to look at Richard sitting next to her, "…and Deb and Quinn and the guys that work for you, whoever they are, went and rescued her…you snatched my baby away from their scummy clutches, not even concerned you all might die; you just went and did it."

Belvia stopped and shrugged.

"You guys just went and did it. So, come what may, I'll always be thankful, Mister President. "When my life had turned to agony, the people in this room stood up and did the right thing, not once but twice. I'll be grateful until the day I die. For most people heroes are abstract. I'm sitting in a room with them."

Fidel stood. He walked around the table until he came to the back of Belvia's chair. He bent down and kissed her on the top of the head. Then he walked back to his chair and sat down.

"It's never wrong to do the right thing," He said. "A twenty-one-year-old corporal told me that once."

"How about another round of drinks, Timothy?" Doctor Gonzales said.

Everyone except Richard and Belvia walked to the bar while Timothy refreshed the various glasses.

Richard sat with his right arm around Belvia's shoulder.

"I love you," he whispered.

"I love you, too."

"Want me to bring you guys something?" Timothy shouted across the room.

"Two mojitos, please," Belvia shouted back. Then she grinned. "Do you want anything, honey?"

"I'll have a double, too!" Richard shouted.

"Here's another problem we need to discuss," Timothy said, after everyone had reassembled around the table.

"There are federal marshals looking for you, Richard. They stopped in Poor Joe's last Saturday, inquiring as to your whereabouts and if you had been in Tennessee. And they are looking for someone you called grandpa."

Richard leaned back in his chair and looked at Quinn.

"Chief Strait says they traced you using fingerprints from your cell…Air Force records. And the folks in Franklin, Tennessee, took it personally when you broke out with the help of grandpa. The marshals are on a mission."

Everyone looked at Richard.

"I had planned a little meeting with Amy Hamilton to explain the reason why she should leave the McMillens alone for the rest of her life. Plans went a little awry when a state trooper pulled up behind her car and Amy hurled herself out onto the highway, screaming rape."

He looked at Stanley and Danielle and then at Rose.

"Where is she, by the way?"

Rose Jackson grinned.

"Nevada."

"You're kidding," Stanley said.

"Seriously, made her a deal she couldn't refuse," Rose said. "That's that."

"Well, anyway, Chief Strait is convinced it's just a matter of time before they figure out who grandpa is and they come looking for both of you."

Richard looked at Quinn.

"Thanks, grandpa."

"Welcome, John Allen."

"It's getting late," Doctor Gonzales said, "and I've had four drinks. If it's all right with you, Mister President, I suggest we reconvene our meeting after breakfast. I have an idea."

"I have one, too," Dora said, "a grand idea!"

Fidel looked at his wife with his eyebrows raised.

She grinned and winked at the man she adores.

CHAPTER 52

HOSPITAL DE CARDENAS

Timothy and Stanley stood, looking down the hill through the third story windows, waiting for everyone to assemble, watching the yellow Volkswagen Beetle driving in circles around and around in the parking lot and then coming to a stop and backing up. Sometimes it stalled when shifted into reverse.

"Charles have driving lessons yet?" Stanley asked.

"Not till next spring."

"Won't be necessary," Stanley said. "Look."

The two fathers watched as Timothy's son drove, shifting from gear to gear, Chloe beside him, clapping.

Danielle, Belvia, and Carla entered the room from the elevator.

"Look who's driving," Timothy said to Carla.

"Is that Charles?"

"Yup."

"He can't drive; he doesn't have a driver's license."

Stanley and Timothy laughed.

"I suspect he'll have one soon if Chloe gets her way," Stanley said.

"Who's that in the back seat with Norah?" Belvia asked, some concern in her voice.

Danielle smiled. "Chloe's friend Juan Pedro Rodriguez. He's a tenth grader and Chloe says he's hot."

"I don't know...I guess...I just worry," Belvia replied.

"Chloe and I talked about introducing boys to Norah after

what she's been through. She said, 'Mom, trust me, I won't let anything bad happen, and Norah needs to feel safe. Besides, we're only speaking in Spanish. And, mom, before any guy meets Norah, I'm going to introduce him to Uncle Richard.'"

"That's true," Richard said, entering the room with Quinn and Fidel. The three men walked to the window and looked down.

"Juan is a very polite young man," Richard said, and he grinned.

"Is that your boy driving Chloe's car?" Fidel asked Timothy.

"It is, Fidel."

"Chloe will tell me when Charles is ready for his driver's license."

• • •

Fidel looked at Katie from his chair at the head of the table.

"I met you at Truman's White House on the day of your wedding. I am very sorry your husband has passed, Katie. Doug inspired those around him. My heart grieves because your heart has been hurt."

"Thank you, Fidel. I do miss him. I can feel his presence."

"That's a comfort. A.W. feels Rita. And Vincent Bonifacio told me that you lost your husband last year, Rose. I am sorry."

"I found Jonathon with his treasured trumpet on the bench behind our home. He's the only man I have ever loved, and the void in my heart will never fill, so I just live with it. Thank you, Fidel."

"You're welcome. I heard you found him on a trip to Big Bay, playing his horn in Poor Joe's."

"Yes. The guys weren't happy when I stole him away." Rose smiled.

"I found my wife at Poor Joe's," Fidel said. "I love that old bar. Someday we're all going back."

He paused.

"I met many of you in Key West; you were at the Truman White House for a wedding and I to meet with your president. Even though he is no longer in office, we speak on the phone almost weekly. He called last night; neither of us sleep much. He called and asked what I knew about the Suriname destroyer. I told him I knew some very corrupt individuals were on board that ship. He said he understood that to be true. And then he said, 'Thank you, my friend. Be vigilant; there are suspicions Cuba is somehow involved. Next week, Senator Rogers will introduce a resolution to investigate Cuba. The Russian ambassador to the United Nations will insist on an international investigation of this great tragedy. They are all connected by a common denominator."

Fidel looked up from his cup of dark coffee.

"I am accustomed to battling evil. I admit to thinking that Batista probably was the worst I would encounter. I wish that had been so. I truly am not concerned for the safety of my beloved Cuba. I'm sorry they are looking for you, Richard. Quinn here likes the sport, but he's no spring chicken and needs to take better care. It saddens me that you are all here because of threats and concerns for your safety…and for your children. I look forward to the day when we all gather at Poor Joe's for a joyous event, maybe a wedding reception like you held for Marco and Marciana! I enjoyed that as much as I have anything in my life."

He paused again and glanced at Stanley and Danielle.

"One never knows; I saw Chloe and Charles holding hands, and then, just now, Charles taking driving lessons from her." Fidel smiled. "That would be a party."

Stanley started to say something and then shut his mouth and smiled at Timothy.

"Well, here's the situation, as I see it," Quinn said. "We're safe here and not so much if we leave."

Marco Gonzales cleared his throat.

"I have an idea I hope you will consider," the doctor said, looking around the room.

Everyone nodded.

"Most of us in this room are familiar with Cardenas and the hospital there."

Fidel rubbed his beard. "You saved my life in that little hospital." He looked at Marco, Stanley, and Danielle.

"Three weeks ago, Fidel requested I meet with the minister of health. I learned Hospital de Cardenas is at risk of closing."

"Why?" Stanley asked.

"Staffing. The hospital now has inadequate maternity staff, no emergency room physician, no cardiology staff, and the nursing staff is aging."

He paused.

"The energy, the vitality no longer lives in the hospital," he continued.

"I know the feeling," Stanley muttered.

"You and Danielle could bring the enthusiasm back, my friend," Marco replied.

Fidel smiled and held both hands toward Stanley and Danielle, sitting side by side at the great round table.

"Now I am pleading," Fidel said, "that you help. I ask as a friend in need."

Danielle stood. She walked to Fidel's spot and leaned over the table, resting both elbows on it, her chin in her hands.

Fidel stared back.

"Of course we are going to help!" she said.

Marco exhaled a deep breath.

"We don't have licenses to practice in Cuba," Stanley said.

"Yes, you do," Fidel replied. "Right, Marco?"

Doctor Gonzales reached into his briefcase. He walked around the table, placing licenses to practice on the table:

STANLEY JAMES McMILLEN, R.N. Ph.D.

DANIELLE MARIE McMILLEN, R.N.

Master's in Nursing and O.B.

A.W. BLUE, M.D. General Medico

"I met Doctor McCaferty and Doctor Smith both at Katie's wedding and in Big Bay during my wedding reception. Yesterday, you mentioned they were both retired or soon would be," Marco said to Stanley.

"Both next month," Stanley replied.

"Would you call them, see if we flew them down," Marco nodded toward Quinn, "and gave them a tour, that perhaps they would be convinced to join us?"

"I'll make the calls, but, Fidel, you'll need to be on the line, too."

"Six-thirty tonight should be a good time," Stanley said. "You need to be here, too, A.W."

●●●

Doctor Jack McCaferty had finished hospital rounds and counted the number of days remaining in his head while walking up the stairs to his office. His private line on his desk rang repeatedly.

...give me a damn break...

"Doctor McCaferty."

"This is Fidel Castro calling from Cuba."

"Sure it is," Jack quipped. "What's the deal with Poor Joe's closing, Wendell?"

"Jack."

"Yes?"

"This is Stanley. You really are speaking with Fidel."

"Well, hello, Mister President, why didn't you say so?"

"I did."

"Got me there; been a long day. How are things in Cuba?"

"We need your help at our hospital in Cardenas. Stanley, tell Jack."

"Jack, this is Marco. Hospital de Cardenas has no cardiologist."

"Jack, this is A.W. You and Kathy would love it here."

Jack McCaferty laughed.

"I'm being gang tackled. What's going on? That's the hospital where you guys were attacked, right?"

"Great memory, Jack. The bullet holes are all patched and walls painted," Marco retorted. "We are hoping for the opportunity to impress you and your wife. Quinn said he will send his plane to pick you up at your convenience. Just a quick trip at Mach 2."

"Danielle and I have already signed on, Jack. I'm going to manage the cardiac care unit. Danielle is going to manage O.B.," Stanley said.

"They made me the director of family medicine, Jack," A.W. chimed in.

"I will be the medical director and hospital administrator, Jack," Marco said, "so no problems from administration."

A long pause.

"How about Friday? I have a three-day weekend. I'll talk to Kathy. How about this Friday?"

"The plane will be in Big Bay at 8:00 a.m.," Quinn said.

"Thanks, Jack. Laverne Smith will be coming down, too. He's just waiting to hear the date," Stanley said.

"He'd make a good ER doc for your hospital," Jack commented.

"That's the plan," Marco replied. "If you and your wives like it, that's the plan."

"Jack, this is Fidel again."

"Yes, sir?"

"Tell your wife she will have a home with a view of the ocean she will find beyond belief."

"Now you're talking Kathy's language." Jack laughed. "One problem though."

"What?" everyone said in unison.

"I can't speak Spanish worth a damn."

Another pause.

"That will not be a problem, Doctor McCaferty. We have an expert translator on staff. And you will learn quickly, I am sure," Fidel said.

Those around the table noticed a twinkle in his eyes.

"OK, see you all Friday."

•••

"What translator?" Marco asked.

Fidel pointed toward Stanley.

"I can't speak it either…yet," Stanley stammered.

"Chloe will need a job when she graduates after next month," the president of Cuba said, grinning. "It will be her first government job before she attends University of Habana."

"She's only in the tenth grade, Fidel."

Fidel leaned back in his chair, beaming.

"Your daughter has completed all the studies through the twelfth grade and has been taking university mathematics and economic classes for the past semester."

Stanley sat stunned.

…why the hell didn't someone tell me…

Fidel looked at the dismay on his friend's face.

"She doesn't want anyone to know. It's her secret to tell at her appointed time. She is brilliant, Stanley. Chloe is humble. Marco, here, has an IQ measured at 148." He glanced at his personal physician and smiled.

"I know things, Marco."

"Your daughter's IQ measured at 159. She doesn't know. Chloe said, 'No thank you' when the professor asked if she wanted to know the results. He asked her why, and she smiled and shook her head no."

"It doesn't really matter, Professor," she said. "I don't want a number to define me."

"The professor is quite impressed."

Danielle sat next to her husband. She held his hand and smiled.

"Does that night nurse still work at the hospital? What was her name – the one who hit on my husband?" Danielle asked Doctor Gonzales.

"She was a naughty one that night!" Fidel said.

Fidel's chief of staff reached into his wallet and retrieved a picture.

"Rhea," he said, handing the picture down the table. "She's a stay-at-home mother…my wife."

"Something good came from that night." Fidel grinned. "Your husband is safe, Danielle."

"I really wasn't worried."

CHAPTER 53

THAT REAL ESTATE AGENT
AND THE TOUR GUIDE

The sun's crest barely peeked over the tall hills east of Big Bay. Drs. McCaferty and Smith walked alongside their wives, Kathy and Mary, toward the idling plane, its turbines whining gently, waiting. Six men dressed in black slacks and black T-shirts, concealing bullet-proof vests, surrounded the sleek, white jet with a needle-nose and swept back wings, holding automatic weapons.

"O'Malley's always on guard," Laverne Smith said to Jack, pointing at the man standing near the plane's open door.

"Likely why he's still alive," Jack replied.

"Hope this doesn't portend our future," Laverne said, walking up the entry ramp.

"I think we'll enjoy this adventure, Laverne. The thought of watching our lives twitter away, going to the Friday medical conferences, sitting at the Muppet's table with the old guys, depresses me. I'd rather flame out in a blaze of glory than shuffle around following a walker."

"Wow! Look at this." Doctor Smith ran his hand over the lounge seats and inhaled the leather smells. "You told me Quinn's plane is special."

"The only one ever built. He'll tell you the story if you ask him." Kathy and Mary sat together.

"What in the world are we going to do in Cuba if our husbands decide to stay?" Mary asked, watching the ground move outside the plane.

"I'm taking this one day at a time," Kathy replied. "Jack hasn't made a wrong decision in the forty-five years I've known him."

The force of acceleration startled the ladies.

"Feels like taking off in the Rocking Rollercoaster at Disney World!" Mary exclaimed.

The 1,500-mile trip from Big Bay to Cardenas took sixty-eight minutes.

Fidel looked up at the plane flying overhead, circling once before swooping down sharply for a landing. He covered his ears when the plane's reverse thrusters roared past him.

The door opened. Three men dressed in green military uniforms pushed an exit ramp against the plane. Fidel handed his cane to his chief of staff and walked with excitement into the plane.

He walked inside and smiled.

"I thank you for coming to Cardenas, Mary and Kathy." He stopped in front of the ladies. "The support you show your husbands made them the great physicians they are. I hope you find our city as friendly as it is beautiful. If you need anything while you are here, please call me."

Fidel continued, "I recall you liked planting and gardens, Mary. I have a gardener who will introduce you to our tropical plants."

"You sent me a note, thanking me for the coffee beans I left for you when I visited Big Bay," Fidel said to Kathy.

"That coffee tasted delicious. I can't replicate it," Kathy said, looking up at the old man.

"And those beans were stale. Wait until you taste freshly roasted beans…from your own coffee plants!"

Kathy smiled.

He handed each lady a presidential card with his phone number.

"Jack and Laverne, it has been a long time since Key West. I am honored that you are here."

"Thanks for the invite," Jack replied, shaking hands.

"This is very gracious of you, inviting us down, Mister President," Laverne said, shaking hands.

"The honor is mine. Unless you prefer to be addressed as Doctor, I would prefer you call me Fidel."

"Thank you, Fidel," Doctor Smith answered, and he smiled.

Dora, Belvia, Katie, Carla, Moses, and Danielle greeted Mary and Kathy when they reached the tarmac.

"You ladies gonna love it here!" Moses exclaimed, her Caribbean blue eyes smiling.

"I read on the trip down that Cardenas is referred to as the Charleston of the Caribbean," Kathy said.

"I don't know 'bout no Charleston. All I know be what I see, and you ladies gonna love dis place."

Dora approached and hugged them both.

"It's been too long," Dora said.

"How's life as Mrs. Castro?" Mary asked.

"I absolutely adore that man," Dora said, watching Fidel in the middle of the men, chatting. "I wish the world knew the man I know."

"We do," Kathy said. "You're right."

"First, before we go to the hospital, I have arranged for a tour of the city and then out to the Hicacos Peninsula," Juan Castro said, interrupting the various conversations. "There is a beautiful little town named Varadero I think you will like."

"On the peninsula Juan will point out the homes that are available," Fidel said. Then he added, "My chief of staff never dreamed his duties would include working as a real estate agent."

Juan smiled and nodded his head at Fidel. "OK, everyone aboard the presidential bus."

The Mercedes-Benz bus toured the narrow downtown streets first and then the residential areas and past the cement block hospital painted blue with HOSPITAL de CARDENAS in white letters above the entrance.

"We'll return here tomorrow," Marco said, and the bus headed north along the marina and out onto the peninsula.

"Look at that beach," Kathy said. "The sand is white!"

Fidel put his weathered hand with age spots over his mouth, hiding his smile. He winked at Jack.

They traveled the eleven miles to the end of the peninsula. From time to time, Marco pointed out homes along the beach which were available.

"How much is that one?" Mary pointed at a rose-colored residence with a red tile roof.

"Oh, I thought you knew. Housing is provided for employees of Hospital de Cardenas. With our compliments," Marco replied. "It is included as part of your earnings."

"Cool," Jack said. Kathy looked at him and smiled.

The bus headed south toward the mainland. Partway back, it turned right, stopping in front of a large pink beach hotel.

HOTEL QUATRO PALMAS

"I hope you enjoy the hospitably of this fine hotel," Fidel said. "I have reserved a private dining room for dinner this evening at 7:00. Please make yourselves comfortable. For lunch, you will find several restaurants. Please tell them you are guests of the president."

He paused.

"It's come to this, Juan…you selling houses and me a tour guide."

"Look at the bright side, Fidel," Jack chuckled, "you have employment opportunities after retirement."

Fidel laughed hard.

"See everyone at 7:00," the president of Cuba said, still smiling.

● ● ●

"What do you think?" Jack asked Kathy, sitting next to his wife on the hotel balcony, looking down at the blue Bay of Cardenas.

"Everyone is so friendly," she replied. "It doesn't feel like an act, either."

"It's a great opportunity, going from the hectic up north practice to this. I'd already begun to feel an empty feeling, seeing the final day coming closer. I think this opportunity is a gift for a job well done, honey."

"I do, too, Jack."

"Guess I'll need Spanish lessons. I remember Danielle gave Stanley some CDs a long time ago; wonder if he still has them?"

"Danielle told me on the bus that Chloe has you enrolled in her Spanish class along with Stanley and Laverne. Stanley never took the CDs out of the box."

"Chloe teaches Spanish?"

"She teaches English at the high school on Nueva Gerona, Danielle told me."

"Smart young lady."

"And the apple of Fidel's eye. He bought her a VW Beetle for her sixteenth birthday."

"I think we are going to like it here," Jack said. "I wonder if they have cigars down in the lobby shop."

"Oh, Jack, you're not going to start smoking cigars. By the way, Mary said Laverne is excited to be part of all this. He's going to do it."

"Grand," Jack said, watching three young boys building a sand castle on the beach with a sand wall to protect it from the rising tide. "That's grand."

● ● ●

Seven courses, not counting dessert. Dinner took three hours on the private patio dining room, illuminated solely by bamboo torches.

"Dis be da best flan; better dan even mine," Moses exclaimed at 10:30. She left the table briefly in search of the chef. She returned, smiling.

Fidel had surprised Chloe's parents, again. While the bus toured the city and peninsula, he had Chloe flown in his personal helicopter from Nueva Gerona to Cardenas. Everyone had been seated, waiting for the president, when he appeared with Chloe on his right arm.

"Let me introduce your interpreter for tomorrow's visit to Hospital de Cardenas," he said, his wrinkled, whiskered face beaming, "and your official Spanish instructor."

"She's grown so much in just the past few months," Mary said, leaning into Laverne.

"Danielle and Chloe look like sisters," Laverne said back, watching Chloe greet each individual at the table, going from person to person. "They're the same size now."

Kathy whispered to Jack, "She is so poised."

"I'm very happy to say everyone has agreed to help keep our little hospital alive," Doctor Gonzales said, standing next to Fidel's chair. "Mister President has personally signed the appropriate licenses to practice in Cuba for each of you."

He smiled and glanced at Chloe. "And you each have a Cuban driver's license with a presidential seal in your welcoming basket being delivered yet this evening."

"It's like a get-out-of-jail card!" Chloe said, from her seat next to her mother. "Or, at least a second chance for speeding, right, Uncle Richard?"

Richard nodded.

"Marciana has accepted a position at the hospital," Marco said, smiling at his wife. "She's the comptroller. Doctor Smith has accepted the position of emergency room director. Doctor McCaferty is now the director of cardiology. Doctor Blue will oversee the walk-in-clinic. Danielle will manage the obstetrics department. Stanley will, of course, head the cardiac care unit."

He looked at Belvia Chase.

"Right before dinner, I asked Belvia if she would consider being my personal secretary. I am happy to say she has accepted."

Chloe clapped. Then everyone clapped and Belvia smiled, her eyes filled with emotion.

"How life happens is an amazing mystery to me," Fidel said. "How things occur, seemingly random events…Stanley and Danielle…Quinn and the Green Parrot Bar."

"I was there, too," Chloe whispered to her mom.

"Shush!" Danielle whispered back.

"If Quinn hadn't taken Rita and me to Cayo Coco," Doctor Blue interjected, "all those many years ago, Norah likely would not have been rescued from St. Kitts. That horrible grief after Rita's passing, it drove me out to sea every evening to say goodnight to her and talk with the dolphins. No accident of fate; I understand now. Norah would need me to be there at that exact moment."

Richard Elmore Fortin listened. He glanced at Quinn who winked back. Then he bowed his head and listened with his eyes closed.

"Thank you, my friends, for helping now," Fidel said. "Cardenas is a special place, the city where the Cuban flag first flew. This hospital is special to me for all the reasons you already know. I am grateful to each of you. Thank you for agreeing even before your visit to the hospital. You are truly friends."

He looked at Stanley and Danielle.

"FINALLY!" he exclaimed. "Finally, after all the years of nearly begging, you are here. I couldn't be happier at this moment," the old man said, looking at everyone.

CHAPTER 54

DORA'S

Following breakfast, the ladies watched their men, accompanied by Belvia, Marciana, and Danielle, leave for the hospital in the Mercedes bus followed by a military Jeep.

Richard, Timothy, and Quinn sat near the beach, discussing something. Quinn answered his Comstat phone.

"I have an idea to show you," Dora said, watching the Jeep turn right and disappear. She turned to her security agent.

"We need a ride," she instructed.

"Yes, madam." He gave instructions into a microphone attached to his shoulder strap.

An armored, three seat Hummer drove around the circle drive.

"May I go, too?" Machete asked, stroking Little Miss.

"It wouldn't be the same without you," Dora said, touching his hand. "Please come."

The ladies climbed into the big green machine. Debra helped Machete climb into the seat behind the driver and closed the door after Little Miss jumped in. She walked around the rear of the Hummer and then backed up. Briefly she stared at a bullet hole in the right rear fender. She said nothing.

The driver looked at Dora.

"Lai-Lai on Avenida Tra," she instructed, twisting back and facing the passengers. "You're going to love this."

The two-story masonry restaurant, painted white with red trim, appeared on the right. It had a flat roof and large fireplace chimney;

and was separated from the street by a white concrete fence with red pillars every twenty feet.

"In here," Dora said, pointing toward the driveway and parking lot.

"It be closed," Moses said, climbing out the passenger side door.

"It's for sale!" Dora exclaimed. "You guys want to help me run it?"

An Asian man and young lady opened the front door.

"Do come in," he said.

"Your husband knows about this?" Rose asked, shaking her head.

"Not yet!"

Moses turned in a slow circle, gazing from the center of the modest dining room.

"What you think, honey?" she asked Machete.

"It is beautiful, Moses. Dora, it feels beautiful."

Moses trotted to the kitchen area then reappeared, grinning. "You gotta see dis stove!"

Dora smiled.

"What's upstairs?" Carla asked.

"Apartments."

Carla and Dora moved closer, face-to-face.

"You want to recreate Poor Joe's, don't you?" Carla said.

"I sure do. I miss it. Will you guys help me?"

"I'll be the greeter!" Machete exclaimed.

"Poor Joe's be closed until de right time it be open!" Moses said, bubbling with excitement. "Want to hear de perfect menu?"

Dora said, "I sure do. Timothy told me. I sure do."

"What are you going to name it?" Carla asked.

"I think DORA'S would be perfect," Rose commented.

Dora looked at her friends for several seconds.

"I like the way that sounds, Rose. DORA'S it is!"

"We need a piano," Carla said.

"And a popcorn machine," Moses added.

"And booths along that wall," Kathy said. "It needs booths."

···

They sat together in a small conference room after touring the hospital.

"First thing that needs to be done is to patch those leaks, Fidel," Jack said, pointing to a rusty bucket in the corner.

"I didn't know."

"Let's make a list." Marco took a pen from his shirt pocket and began numbering a legal pad.

"First the roof," Jack repeated. "We can't have contaminated water dripping down on us."

"We need to expand the CCU from two beds to four. Can we remove the west wall between rooms?" Stanley added.

"If we separate the ER from the walk-in traffic with less serious problems, we can make it work," Laverne Smith added.

"We need a landing pad for a helicopter," Jack said. "There are times when we'll need to transfer acute cases to Havana."

Marcos wrote each suggestion on his pad. He looked at Fidel.

"I'll find the financing," Fidel said, "somewhere." He rubbed his beard.

…he looks tired, Stanley thought.

The conference door squeaked open. The men looked up, watching a grim-faced Quinn, followed by Timothy and Richard, enter the room.

"We have a bad problem in Nicaragua," Quinn said.

…he's frightened, Danielle thought, watching Quinn's ashen face. *I've never seen him scared.*

"Received a call from my contact with the UN's World Health Organization." He looked at Drs. Smith and McCaferty then Marco, Stanley, and A.W.

"There's an epidemic spreading in Nicaragua. The epicenter appears to be Matagalpa. It's spreading downstream following the river, now in San Nicolas and San Juanillo."

*…Richard looks like hell…*Stanley felt tightness in his neck.

"What kind of epidemic?" Laverne asked.

Quinn took a deep breath before answering.

"Coven Pharmaceuticals had a research and development lab in Matagalpa. They had developed an aberrant H1N3 flu virus and infected a mutated mosquito as a carrier. They intentionally infected a small village in South Africa with devastating results – eighty percent mortality; the virus causes systemic arterial inflammation. Cause of death, regardless of age, is usually myocardial infarction, stroke, or kidney failure."

He paused and looked at the wide eyes staring back at him, faces fading color to ashen.

"Coven Pharmaceuticals is owned by the world cartel known as The Company. This group controls drug cartels and human trafficking around the world; same group that ran the St. Kitts sex business."

Doctor Blue became more pale. Belvia visibly trembled. A.W. held her hand.

"We think they developed this virus for two purposes. First, to start an epidemic and then to develop an effective vaccine and save the world, achieving hero status while making billions. Second, as a biological weapon of mass destruction, a powerful threat to governments, especially third world countries whose law enforcement agencies might object to their operations."

Richard moved next to Quinn. He said, "Amy Hamilton worked as a drug rep for Horizon Pharmaceuticals, who also owns Coven. We had occasion to discuss her future not long ago; she admitted to being more than a drug rep. She told Quinn and me the mutated virus and hybrid mosquito had problems. They were having trouble keeping the hybrid mosquito alive long enough for it to be an effective weapon."

Richard looked at Quinn.

"Just before we joined you on Nueva Gerona, we destroyed the R&D lab in Matagalpa. We used an incendiary bomb, believing all life forms would be obliterated."

"The bug somehow survived and has mutated again. Now the hybrid mosquitoes are breeding and transmitting the virus."

The room became silent.

"It infects children?" Fidel finally spoke.

"Especially children," Quinn replied.

"Do we know, have they developed a vaccine?" Lavern asked.

Quinn shook his head no. "When asked, all the pharmaceutical companies express great alarm and know nothing. But they do have a desire to help and want serum samples from the victims."

"Which mosquito?" Jack inquired.

"Tiger."

"We're in trouble."

"I bet Amy knows."

Everyone turned to look at Stanley.

"I bet Amy knows if a vaccine is developed," Stanley repeated. "She always has known more than she lets on."

"Rose has her tucked away in Reno...new identity," Quinn said.

"Well, let's ask Rose and pay her a visit," Richard said, nodding at Quinn.

"This time I go, guys."

Every head turned toward Stanley again.

"Amy and I have known each other since junior high. We loved each other in high school. This time I'll talk with her. We can't have her angry."

Stanley paused and looked at Quinn and Richard.

"Trust me, we don't want her angry," Danielle said with a tone only Stanley understood.

She reached to the tabletop and grasped her husband's hand. It felt cold.

The only sound in the room came from the ceiling water drip... drip...dripping in the rusty bucket.

"She's right about that," Richard said.

CHAPTER 55

HEARTS BEATING IN UNISON

"I love you more than I can put into the right words." Danielle snuggled close to Stanley. She spoke softly in his ear.

He squeezed her body tightly.

"I can feel your heart beating," he whispered.

"Let's lie here and see if we can get our hearts to beat in unison," she whispered. "We used to do that when we were dating."

"I loved that."

They lay together on top of the hotel bed sheets, listening to the waves from the Bay of Cardenas crashing on the beach not far away, washing away the sand castle the three little boys had built at low tide.

"You know I hate the idea of you going to Amy."

"Yup. I would hate it if you had to see Jeff Prudhomme."

She rolled back just a little, far enough to look at his face. "How do you know about Jeff?"

Stanley grinned and shrugged. "Quinn."

"I think I'll slap that man."

"Quinn or Jeff?"

Danielle put her lips on Stanley's.

Looking down, Danielle whispered, "Can you feel it? We're doing it. Our hearts are beating exactly together!"

They lay pressed together, listening to the waves for a long time.

"I felt sorry for Fidel tonight at dinner. Dora is so excited with her plans to open a restaurant. Moses made it even worse, being all bubbly like she is, talking about this recipe and that and the best flan in the world. I could see the excitement in Carla's eyes, too. They are so excited. But, I felt sorry for Fidel. He tried so hard to seem excited. It must be awful some days, being a president," Danielle said.

"I watched Machete. Did you see the look on that little Mexican's face? He listened and petted Little Miss, faster and faster. I can tell he knows something is wrong."

"How does he do that?"

"Don't know. He told me once he can see the color of blackness. That's his explanation. He can see evil."

"That would be awful, too, I think," Danielle said. "Why don't you take Machete with you?"

"I want you to come with me to Reno," Stanley replied.

"You don't need me there to do the job you need to do," she replied, squeezing even tighter.

"I'll ask him in the morning," Stanley said. "I wonder how Katie is doing back at the compound, the lone adult among all those children?"

"I asked Chloe. She said Katie and Lina drive to the market every morning for produce and then Katie reads in the afternoon. She's going through Fidel's library; just finished *The Old Man and the Sea* and started *Of Mice and Men.* She plays dominoes with the kids after school and is learning Spanish."

Danielle and Stanley hugged close, watching the red sky fade to darkness before they slept, their hearts beating in unison.

CHAPTER 56

THE EGG DRAWER

"I'm not sure that she'll be able to help," Rose said, walking on the white sand beach alongside Stanley.

Stanley watched her face.

"Why?"

"You noticed I left for a few days?"

"I did."

They stopped at a yellow cabana and sat in the chairs.

"Made a deal with Amy. She gets the hell out of your lives and I get her a new identity – new social security number, driver's license, the works. She agreed, out of fear for her life. Quinn took care of all the documents. I set her up to be the manager for one of my gentlemen's clubs in Reno. Five days ago one of the ladies called me, worried about Sandi; that's her new name, Sandi Amelia. She told me Sandi had been vomiting and complaining about a bad headache and needing glasses. They found her in the office, on the floor, unconscious. That's when I flew back."

Stanley cupped his hands and blew into them, staring at the rough waves and their whitecaps.

"Sounds like a tumor, Rose."

Rose smiled. "You sure know a bunch of stuff. Glioblastoma."

"Shit."

"Doctor Maser took her to surgery; removed as much of the tumor as she dared. Amy's awake now that the pressure is relieved."

"She conversant?"

"As much as I detested her, I feel sorry for her."

Stanley looked up from his cupped hands.

"Stanley, she's simple minded now. Amy thinks I'm her mother; kept calling me mom. And…"

She looked at Stanley with sad, blue eyes.

"…she cries almost all the time because her husband left her."

"Which one?"

"You. She thinks you're her husband."

Stanley leaned forward, his forehead buried in the palms of both hands. He thought for several minutes before looking up, tilting his head just enough to look at Rose with his left eye.

"This complicates things."

"No kidding," Rose replied.

"I still have to try."

• • •

Chloe glanced at her mother's face and then back toward Quinn's Gulfstream, watching Machete and Little Miss going through the jet's door. Quinn and Richard stood beside them, not saying a word.

"You really can't say what they're up to, can you?" Chloe said as the jet roared past and then upward steeply.

Danielle looked at Quinn and shrugged a tentative shrug.

Richard finally spoke.

"You remember the plagues in the old testament?" he said.

"Sure, especially the Egyptian plagues when Jehovah became angry."

"Your daddy is on his way to stop one."

"He's my hero, you know. You should be with him," Chloe responded.

"I would like nothing more. This one he has to do alone."

"Machete will keep an eye on things," Chloe said, walking toward the car.

•••

"Rose Jackson called to tell me you were coming and to share Sandi's medical information with you," Doctor Maser said, looking up at Stanley.

"I've known her a long time. What's her status?"

"Thirty millimeter grade four glioblastoma, left occipital area. I resected all I dared. She's had a slow post-op bleed. The drain is still in; intracranial pressure now within normal limits."

"MRI show mets?"

"Has metastasized to the brainstem and spine."

Stanley looked into the young neurosurgeon's brown eyes.

"She doesn't have much longer."

"I'm not sure she'll last the day out," Doctor Maser replied. "It's good you came when you did."

She looked at Stanley with a curious expression.

"She believes you're her husband."

"Rose told me, and that Rose is her mom."

"Happens with brain injuries, you know."

"Had one myself doctor. OK if we go in now?" Stanley looked through the room's glass door.

"Sure."

"I'm going to hug my wife," he said softly. Stanley turned, reached down and guided Little Miss and Machete through the door and then closed it.

•••

Amy Hamilton's swollen face turned toward Stanley.

"Hi, honey, you came back! Why'd you leave me? I don't know why you left me. I love you so much!"

Machete sat in a chair in the far corner of the room, next to the sink.

"I love you, too," Stanley said, bending over the side rail, kissing her on the forehead.

"You remember that night after the sophomore dance? That's the first time you kissed me."

"That was a very special night," Stanley replied, uncovering her hand and holding it.

"Please hold me."

Stanley looked up at Machete in the corner. Machete nodded his head yes.

Stanley put the side rail down.

"Where've you been, anyway? I've been so worried," Amy said.

"I've been looking for it," Stanley replied, lying next to Amy.

A nurse came into the room to replace an IV bottle. Machete motioned to the young lady and whispered something in her ear. She smiled and pulled the curtain closed when she left.

Amy lay her bandaged head on Stanley's chest.

"I can hear your heart beating."

"Let me know if it stops."

"You make me happy. I'm glad you came back."

"I still need to find it, honey. The kids are getting sick in Nicaragua."

"You know! It's in the refrigerator, in the egg drawer."

"I forgot."

"It's always been in the egg drawer. You told me not to trust them."

"I remember now. The egg drawer in New York."

"I'm tired. I love you. I love you."

Stanley twisted his head and looked at her blackened eyes.

"I have always loved you," she said with her eyes closed.

Stanley listened to Amy's breathing becoming shallower and irregular. He watched the cardiac monitor showing sinus tachycardia then slowing…slowing…slowing, finally deteriorating to an agonal rhythm.

Amy's body quivered with a little seizure and then Stanley felt her melting into him.

He lay beside her for a long time with his eyes closed.

● ● ●

"Quinn, find Amy Hamilton's condo in New York City," Stanley said, holding his yellow Comstat phone, standing on the porch of a Reno motel. Machete sat next to him.

"OK, what's there?"

"Look in the refrigerator's egg compartment. I think the vaccine is in the egg drawer."

"You sound like shit, Stan."

"I hope I never have to do anything like that again."

"Rough, huh?"

"Sandi Amelia died in my arms today."

Stanley slumped down on the chair next to Machete.

"Glorious brightness…" Machete hesitated, waiting for a loud semi-truck to pass on the interstate. "…only pure love…no darkness at all."

Little Miss repeatedly licked Stanley's arm.

CHAPTER 57

NEVER AGAIN

"I felt it when you laid beside her."

"Machete said he saw only brightness."

The waves grew larger, washing warm saltwater over their feet and up around the yellow cabana.

"Yesterday afternoon I sat right here," Danielle said, "listening to the waves repeat your name over and over...*Stanley...Stanley... Stanley.* It started like a fever but warmer inside, and for a second I felt afraid, but then I could feel your heart beating, asking for help and I whispered, 'yes.' For a little while three hearts beat together and then just you and me again."

"What time?"

"Four thirty-five. I looked."

"That's when Amy died."

"What happened to her?"

"Glioblastoma, grade four with mets."

"Wonder how much that changed her personality. She certainly could not have been the girl you loved in high school."

"I didn't know the person she'd become. When she showed up at the hospital, working as a drug company representative...she wasn't the Amy I knew."

"You did the right thing, honey. Her last memory being held by her high school lover."

"The hardest thing I've ever done. I looked at Machete when she died. He stared at me with his brown eyes, and I swear he could see me. Janet Sue sat next to him. Until my dying day, I'll have that image of Machete, Little Miss, and Janet Sue sitting in a row next to the sink, and Amy's body feeling heavier and heavier."

"She came to take your friend back home."

"Yup, I think so, too."

"I don't ever want to share you like that again."

"Me too, sweetheart, me too."

Stanley fumbled in his shirt pocket for the vibrating phone. He glanced at the triangular phone's screen.

"Hi, Quinn."

"Actually, she had a West Street Battery Park hotel suite, overlooking the Statue of Liberty."

"Impressive. Did you find the vaccine?"

"Both vaccine and serum labeled *South Africa*."

"Whew!"

"And there's even better news."

"I'm ready."

"The guys in the lab have come up with a concoction that kills the resistant hybrid tiger mosquito! A mixture of malathion, pyrethrin, and DDT kills the little buggers. Being delivered to the Nicaraguan Air Force tomorrow."

Stanley sat silently, listening to the waves.

"You still there?"

"Don't have any words right now, Quinn."

"Been quite a month. Hang in there, buddy."

"Fidel know?"

"He's standing right here."

"In New York?"

"Said he hadn't seen it since he visited the United Nations years ago."

"You guys are nuts. Don't get caught."

"Neither one of us gives a damn, Stan."

CHAPTER 58

BE ALL NIGHT!

Machete sat, leaning forward, in a wicker chair on the porch. A line of eager locals snaked through the parked cars from the porch through the dimly lit parking lot all the way to the sidewalk on the street.

The illuminated sign hanging from the second story simply proclaimed DORA'S in bold neon red letters.

Pete and Wayne had already established their residence at a little round table next to the old upright piano.

To their amazement, the customers watched their president sitting with Juan Castro and A.W. Blue at a corner table.

"He never is in the public like now," an old man said to his daughter, in Spanish.

"His new wife has changed him," the young lady with long black hair answered.

From their booths, the McCafertys and Smiths watched Timothy behind the bar, shaking mojitos.

The teenagers claimed the corner booth next to the popcorn machine. Charles and Juan periodically filled red and white popcorn buckets, placing them on the tables for new customers while Chloe and Norah watched and grinned at each other.

Quinn, Vincent Bonifacio, and Rose sat with Stanley and Danielle next to Fidel's table.

Every once in a while, Moses' face would appear from the kitchen to assess the crowd.

"They be happy!" she reported to Dora.

At 10:00 p.m. Moses wiggled through the crowd to the porch. She watched her husband shake hands and listened to him softly say "Bienvenido" to each person entering.

...love that Machete...I be a fortunate girl...

"I hope we have plenty of de foods," Moses exclaimed to an exhausted Dora.

"Why do you say that?" Dora asked, while wiping her forehead with a bar towel.

"We gonna be here all night, Miss Dora."

Carla winked at her husband from the piano bench.

Every once in a while, the percussive sounds from a helicopter could be heard coming from high overhead.

CHAPTER 59

FEELS LIKE HOME

"I can't remember the last time we didn't go to bed." Stanley cupped his hands and splashed cold water on his face for the second time. Danielle walked into the small bathroom and handed him a cup of Bustelo coffee. She held both hands in the running water and rubbed her cheeks.

"Me either. Maybe a shower'll help. That was quite a grand opening."

"After your shower, let's take a ride out the peninsula; something I want to show you."

"I'll just want to go to bed if I take a shower. Let's go."

Stanley grinned.

"Forget it, mister. I'd sleep through it and you'd have to leave me a note, letting me know how it was."

They walked through the hotel parking lot, holding hands.

"Sure is nice of Fidel giving us a car; what kind is it?"

"A Russian name I can't pronounce. Looks like a Packard."

"If you say so. You missing your Avanti?"

They drove north.

"You realize it was seventeen years ago this month we went with Quinn to Cuba for the very first time?" Danielle asked.

"Guess you're right. Chloe's sixteen now. Hadn't thought about it."

"I was so scared and excited, taking off to a forbidden island with Quinn O'Malley."

Stanley smiled. "You didn't show it. You made me brave."

Danielle leaned her head on Stanley's shoulder and closed her eyes. "We've been doing that for each other ever since we met."

Stanley turned right and drove up a long driveway over a sand dune. The car stopped next to a white house with red tile roofing.

"What do you think?"

Danielle looked all around. She smiled.

They walked together, looking room to room and then finally slid the glass doors open, leading to a deck which extended over the sand dune. They walked out, looking at the Atlantic Ocean and several palm trees.

"It feels like our home," Danielle said.

"I thought you'd like it. Raul saved it for us."

"You ready to start all over in a ramshackle Cuban hospital?" Danielle asked.

She put her arms around Stanley's waist and squeezed him from behind.

"I am if you are," he replied, leaning back and kissing her on the cheek.

"You never answered my question."

"Which one?"

"You miss your Avanti?"

"We'll take it for a ride on vacation next summer."

CHAPTER 60

A MUSSED-HAIRED MAN

A black London taxi maneuvered through the traffic on Moorgate Street. The shiny car pulled to the curb and stopped. Two men climbed from the rear seat. The man wearing a blue-striped Armani suit turned back, extending his arm through the open passenger's window, handing the driver fifty dollars, U.S. Then they took the elevator to the top floor of the tall building.

"Sorry we're late…London traffic," the man in the Armani said to a mussed-haired man smoking a cigarette, sitting at the head of the table.

"Let's get started…now," the man replied sarcastically, lighting a fresh cigarette with the butt of the spent one. "I call this meeting to order. Ronald will start with a status report."

"There's no question that our various enterprises have been disrupted. The True Believers, the Italians in Minneapolis, the Cubans led by crazy Fidel, have impacted our cash flow, short term. We have lost key people, but, as we know, no one is indispensable or irreplaceable…different faces, new ideas."

The man named Ronald spoke with a South African accent.

Ronald continued, "We have learned not to have all the eggs in one basket. Joan has replaced Ivan as our human resources director." He nodded in her direction.

Joan said, "Having our entire human resources located in St. Kitts proved to be a critical infrastructure weakness. We are diversifying with clinics now in Toledo, Toronto, San Cristóbal, and, soon, Bangkok."

"We suffered severe setbacks in Nicaragua," the mussed-haired man said in the direction of the young man wearing the Armani suit. "We'd like an update."

"Nicaragua ends up being a blessing in disguise," the man replied. "We were struggling to keep the mosquitoes viable and useful. Our scientists in Hong Kong have mutated the bird flu virus H3N7. Infected chickens show no sign of illness while spreading the virus bird to bird and through their eggs. It spreads easily to humans through eggs, causing a viral pneumonia which is lethal. And, we have developed a vaccine…trialed it in Changsha, China, nearly 100-percent effective. We're back in business, an epidemic waiting to happen."

"Great news," the chain smoker said, stuffing another cigarette butt into a small glass ashtray, forcing several butts to spill onto the shiny tabletop. "In the past, we held our meetings at remote locations, believing anonymity in the third world would provide protection. In retrospect, that is exactly what our enemies wanted, no real protection provided from the local authorities."

He lit another cigarette.

"It is better, I think, to hide in plain sight, right here in London, one of the most security conscious places on earth. There are cameras everywhere, watching everyone. O'Malley and his band of merry men will hesitate to attack us here."

"It's not here that concerns me," a man from Calcutta sitting across the table from Joan said. "Those guys will stalk us like a mongoose following a snake. This committee does not have a good track record for longevity," he concluded.

The smoking man scratched the cowlick above his left ear, mussing his hair more, before reaching into a brown, leather briefcase.

"Legitimate concern," he replied. "And here's how we neutralize that. A cook at Castro's place on the Isle of Youth informed me of a young lady who's the apple of Fidel's eye and the goddaughter to O'Malley. She currently lives in Cardenas with her parents. This September she leaves for the University of Havana."

He put the cigarette down and passed out a photograph.

"They'll agree to anything," he snarled, "when her sobbing voice comes over the phone."

"Pretty girl," the man in the blue-striped Armani suit said. "What's her name?"

"Very pretty," the smoker replied, rubbing the last cigarette out.

"Her name is Chloe Norma McMillen."

EPILOGUE

"The sky is blank but beautiful.
Nothing will ever be the same –
a cup of emptiness to fill,
symbols shaped into a name."

RACHEL HADAS

To be continued…

Richard Alan Hall lives in Traverse City, Michigan with
his wife, Debra Jean, and their three dogs: Thelma,
Hayden, and a red-haired hussy named Lucy. He writes
in Traverse City and in Key West, Florida.